"I'm still scared to go home and face everybody,"
Janet said, picking up a piece of bread.
"But I know it's the right thing to do.
The Hatchery is where I belong."

As she started to bring the bread to her mouth, a deep
wailing cry filled the air. Janet froze, the bread halfway
to her mouth. The sound was mournful, a lone voice
calling across the mist. It echoed in the fog, surrounding Janet and Zephyr.

Then it was quiet again. Janet held her breath but
heard only the soft dripping of rainwater off the leaves
of the trees.

"What was that?" Janet asked in a hushed whisper.

"Not certain," answered Zephyr, straightening up.
She stretched her neck high, turning her head from
side to side as if to catch the fading sound in her ears.

Janet started as the cry rose again. Deeper and
more hollow this time.

VISIT THE EXCITING WORLD OF

IN THESE BOOKS:

DINOTOPIA®
HATCHLING

by Midori Snyder

BULLSEYE BOOKS

Random House 🏠 New York

To my daughter,
Taiko,
with love
—MS

Special thanks to
paleontologist Michael Brett-Surman, Ph.D.,
James Gurney, and Scott Usher.

A BULLSEYE BOOK PUBLISHED BY RANDOM HOUSE, INC.

Library of Congress Catalog Card Number: 95-70117

ISBN: 0-679-86984-0

RL: 5.8

Manufactured in the United States of America 10 9 8 7 6 5 4 3

Cover illustration by Michael Welply

HATCHLING

CHAPTER 1

Janet held her nose and squeezed her mouth shut beneath the covers. If she sneezed now, Zephyr would hear her and find her hiding place. Janet was sweating, her brown curls sticking to her neck. Tears leaked from her tightly closed eyes. But she refused to sneeze. She was determined to win the game.

She sniffed quietly to get rid of the sneeze, then froze as she heard someone climbing the stairs to the sleeping quarters where she lay hidden. She went deeper into the rumpled covers of the round nest-shaped bed. Then she grinned into her palm. Zephyr would never find her here. Janet would wait until the last possible moment—until it was too late for Zephyr to escape. Then, leaping up, Janet would catch the dinosaur by surprise and tag her!

Janet strained to follow the muffled sounds in the room. Finally she sensed Zephyr leaning over the bed. Slowly, the covers were being pulled back. Now! she thought with excitement.

Janet leaped up. "You're it!" she cried, flinging

herself toward the dinosaur.

But it wasn't Zephyr. Instead Janet's mother, Emer, stood there. Emer gave a small startled scream and dropped the clean sheets she'd been holding. Janet realized her mistake too late to stop her body from hurtling into her mother's arms.

"Oh, my!" Emer cried.

"Oh, no!" answered Janet. They stumbled backward and collapsed into the pile of fallen sheets. There was a moment of silence. Then from beneath Janet her mother spoke.

"Janet Elizabeth Morgan!" Emer announced. "What do you mean by leaping out at me like that! You've nearly put the heart crosswise in me." Emer sat up as Janet scrambled off her mother. Then Emer asked in a more gentle voice: "Are you hurt any?"

"Oh, Mammie, I'm so sorry! Really I am," Janet apologized. A blush burned across her cheeks. "I was playing a game with Zephyr, and I thought...I thought..." Janet stopped, suddenly aware of the disheveled figure of her usually tidy mother sprawled on the floor amid the sheets. Emer's black hair had unraveled from its careful bun and tumbled over her shoulders in disarray. Her small gold-rimmed spectacles were tilted on her nose, and her petticoats had risen above her knees, showing off her long purple socks. Janet could feel the start of a giggle, but didn't dare let it show.

"And what were you playing?" Emer asked. Her

2

mother was trying to look stern, but Janet saw Emer's green eyes sparkle as she straightened her glasses.

"Hide the Egg," Janet answered.

"And you were—?"

"The egg."

"And are you hatched now, then?" Emer asked, a warm smile lighting her face.

"I expect I am," Janet said, laughing. She was relieved that her mother wasn't angry. Then something else tugged at her attention. Janet's eyes darted around the room. Where was Zephyr? She must have heard the commotion. Where was the dinosaur hiding? After all, the game wasn't over yet.

Emer began to gather the fallen sheets. "Well, my hatchling, it's time you were away to your class. I've heard rumor that Fatherfast is choosing three new apprentices to attend the next hatching. I'm thinking you're to be among them."

"Oh, Mammie, really?" Janet asked, forgetting her game with Zephyr. This was far more important. *This* was what she had spent the last five years of nursery school learning. "Do you really think I'm ready? Even after…" Janet's voice trailed off as she looked around at the mess. She went to pick up the sheets, but her mother stopped her, taking Janet squarely by the shoulders.

"You're a good girl, Janet. It's no wonder that Zephyr chose you as nestfriend, and spoke for you today among the Ovinutrix."

"Zephyr spoke for me?" Janet asked, awed.

"Oh, aye. And a good speech it was, so I'm told." Emer smiled and brushed back the tangle of curls from Janet's face. "You've a bit too much fun in you sometimes, but sure what's the harm? You know when to be serious as well, and I've faith that you will do the job as is needed when the time comes."

Janet sighed, pleased by her mother's words. Then excitement lit her face. She was twelve years old now, nearly thirteen. Only two other students from her class would be chosen to attend the new hatching. After this hatching, she would be a full apprentice with the responsibility of attending dinosaur births and overseeing their care while small.

"I won't disappoint you, Mammie," Janet said softly. "You'll see."

"It's yourself who must be pleased, Janet, my love," Emer replied. "I will always be proud of you. But you must be proud of your own work as well."

"I'll try, Mammie. I'll work hard."

"I know you will," Emer said, and stroked Janet's cheek. "Go on, then, to class. It wouldn't do to turn up late."

"But the mess—"

"Not to worry. I'll do it. I hope the bed holds no more surprises!" her mother added with a smile.

"Thank you." Janet laughed and hurried through the door.

Janet rushed through the twisting corridors of the

sleeping chambers that honeycombed the upper floors of the Hatchery. Different staircases off the corridors went to other parts of the Hatchery below. Janet dashed past a wooden staircase where the sound of singing and banging of pots rose from the kitchen as the midday meal was prepared. Janet passed the stone staircase that led to the quiet libraries and the common sitting rooms where people read and studied.

Finally Janet reached the spiral staircase that led down to the Incubation Room, which would be her classroom until the next hatchings. A thousand thoughts chattered in her mind. She was to be chosen as an apprentice! Soon she would be a full member of the Hatchery. She saw herself in the years to come, loved by dinosaurs and human beings alike for her skill. She would travel, like the Ovinutrix, to all the hatcheries in Dinotopia. Then she could go to Waterfall City and add her knowledge to the written texts in the great libraries.

Distracted by such far-flung visions, Janet didn't see the long narrow shadow of someone hiding behind the door to the Incubation Room. She bolted through the door and was stopped by a hand that grabbed her.

"It!" squeaked a voice, which then bugled in triumph.

Janet whirled to come face to face with Zephyr. The young Dryosaurus glowed with amusement, her scales an iridescent blue and green. Orange patches bloomed above each glittering gold eye. Zephyr couldn't smile, but she looked pleased with herself nonetheless, her long muscular tail held upright proclaiming her success.

"Not fair!" Janet cried as she realized she had been caught daydreaming.

"Fair it is, Janet, nestfriend," crooned Zephyr, and gave a low-throated gargle that was meant as a chuckle. Her scales flashed, and over her eyes the orange patches brightened like small suns. "Your mind sings inward. Doesn't hear outside. Zephyr waits. Easy to catch!"

Janet started to protest, and then stopped, shrugging her shoulders in friendly surrender. "Aye," she agreed, grinning sheepishly at Zephyr. "You're right!"

Zephyr called it mindsinging. Her parents called it daydreaming. Either way it was the same. She stopped listening to the world and stopped taking part in what was going on around her. An apprentice needed to be able to listen so she could hear the first piped songs of the hatchling dinosaur from inside the egg and find out when its hatching would be. Janet worried as she thought of her daydreaming habit.

"Is it well with you?" Zephyr asked, taking Janet's hands between her two long palms. She tilted her head to one side to better view Janet's face. Janet knew the dinosaur was "listening" to unspoken words of Janet's mood. Zephyr's palms were smooth and cool, slowly accepting warmth from Janet's hands.

"Oh, aye," Janet sighed. "I was just wondering…" She paused. Zephyr's face came closer, her fern-scented breath soft on Janet's cheek.

"Sing to me, Janet," Zephyr coaxed, her golden eyes glowing like warm firelight.

"Mammie told me that you spoke for me today. Are you sure I'm ready?"

Zephyr raised her head, her neck gracefully arching in a gesture of respect. She lowered her golden gaze, and her voice rumbled softly. "With certainty. You sing from the heart, Janet. Only remember to listen from the heart too!"

"Thank you," Janet said.

Zephyr shook her head lightly, the sunspots over her eyes shading to a burnished copper. "Look, here they come," she said as the door to the library opened and the other students entered the Incubation Room, followed by the elderly Ovinutrix, Fatherfast. "Listen for your name, Janet!" Zephyr gave her a quick pat and slipped away to the far rim of the Incubation Room where a few nestfriend dinosaurs had gathered.

The Incubation Room was large, with high ceilings and small windows near the top. A wide doorway opened to a dinosaur resting chamber, and a second doorway led out to the fields. On one wall was a plaster-and-stone fireplace with a huge cauldron resting on a grate inside. Wood was stacked beside the hearth. When the room was used as a classroom, it was filled with long tables and chairs. But today the tables had all been pushed to one side, and large bouquets of flowers were on all the tables. The chairs were tucked out of the way, leaving space for more people than usual.

Students stood in tight knots around Janet, talking excitedly. Over the noisy chatter Janet heard the dinosaurs softly humming the chant of good fortune. Someone laughed, and Janet saw Roberto whispering to a small dark-haired girl named Mariko. Roberto and Mariko were most likely the other two students to be named apprentices. Mariko nodded to Janet. Roberto tossed back his long red hair and gave Janet a bright smile, full of white teeth. On the edges of the room, Zephyr stood next to Rugga and Filo, the nest-friends of Mariko and Roberto. Rugga's scales were a soft moss green next to Filo's burnt yellow scales. Janet grinned at them.

Fatherfast gazed at his students. His head crest was a deep scarlet, and his tail was striped with dark maroon bands. Then he scratched his clawed feet lightly on the floor to begin class. Around him, the human voices quieted.

"Observe, listen, and learn," Fatherfast recited in a scratchy voice. "So it is written in the code of Dinotopia. And so have three of your number done. Observed, listened, and learned. Now has the shell cracked open, and now are they ready to do more. We welcome into our apprenticeship Roberto Falcone, Mariko Nagai, and Janet Morgan."

Even though she was prepared, Janet's heart leaped at the sound of her name. The quiet humming of the three nestfriend dinosaurs bubbled over into a gliding song while a ripple of applause broke out and cheerful congratulations were offered.

None of the students had known when Fatherfast would announce the apprenticeships, but the rest of the Hatchery did. People crowded the doorways, clapping and smiling. Janet's parents were there, as were Roberto's and Mariko's, all looking flushed with pride. In a happy confusion, Janet was hugged and kissed while her hands were squeezed and her hair was ruffled. The larger sauropods had gathered in the resting chamber just beyond the Incubation Room and were filling the chamber with their rumbling dinosaur song. The singing cooks arrived with platters of sweets and laid them on the tables.

Then Fatherfast called everyone back to attention. Gradually, the room quieted once more. The rumbling song of the sauropods echoed like distant thunder off the chamber walls and then fell silent.

"The promise of new life hatches every day," said Fatherfast in his soft reedy voice. "And those already hatched continue to learn and to be reborn, like the sun, which each day breaks open the shell of the horizon anew in order to rise. You three—Roberto, Mariko, and Janet—once students, now begin anew as apprentices. And each egg that hatches under your care will be a gift to remind you of your second hatching at this moment." Fatherfast gave a low breathy sigh and lowered his head. Everyone waited in silence, letting the importance of the occasion settle into their memories. Then Fatherfast lifted his head again, and his crest glowed crimson with emotion. "Breathe deep, seek peace."

Janet stood between Roberto and Mariko as everyone in the Hatchery shook their hands and repeated the Dinotopian saying. Janet's cheeks hurt from smiling, but she was much too happy to stop. Zephyr wiggled through the crowd of well-wishers to pat Janet on the back and stand with her, proud of their friendship.

"Is it well with you?" Zephyr asked, head cocked with worry as tears glistened in Janet's eyes.

"Oh, aye, Zephyr. I always cry when I'm very happy."

Zephyr gave a gargle-sounding laugh. Then she scratched her neck briskly with one claw, her scales flashing a brilliant blue and green.

"And you?" asked Janet, noticing her nestfriend's sudden itch.

"Oh, yes, happy I am too. I always scratch when greatly pleased."

Janet laughed and put her arm around Zephyr's shining neck. She couldn't remember a happier day. She looked at the proud faces of her mother and father and was determined to prove to them that she was worthy of her new position. Fatherfast was the last to congratulate her, holding her hands gently between his small supple fingers. She thought of how many eggs had passed through those fingers, and how many students had stood here, hatched into apprentices by his knowledge and patient teaching. Janet bowed her head to the ancient Ovinutrix, humbled and pleased by his recognition.

"Thank you," Janet said quietly.

"It is the teacher who rejoices in a good student," Fatherfast answered. "I am thankful for you and Roberto and Mariko."

Zephyr gave Janet a nudge. "Janet, come quick. There are good things to eat and much music to sing. Today is for celebration."

"I'm coming, I'm coming, Zephyr," she said, laughing.

Janet threw her arm around Zephyr's neck and headed for the tables. Good smells tickled her nose as the cooks shouldered through the happy crowd bringing more food and tureens of punch. From the resting chambers came the joyful sound of dinosaurs singing.

CHAPTER 2

Three days later, Janet sat beside the hearth of the Incubation Room with Roberto and Mariko, drinking tea out of big mugs. Mia, the older apprentice assigned to help them, had arrived to discuss problems they might have with the eggs during their watch. There were three watches each day, and the new apprentices rotated the hours they were to watch over the eggs, with the help of an experienced apprentice.

On her first day Janet had Sun's Rising, in the morning hours, Roberto had Sun's Falling, in the afternoon, and Mariko had the task of staying awake all night for the third watch, Night's Gathering.

On the second day Janet had been given Sun's Falling, Roberto had gotten Night's Gathering, and Mia had taken Sun's Rising so that Mariko could sleep and have one day off.

"Sleep," groaned Roberto softly at Janet's side. "I need to sleep."

Janet smiled at her friend. Beneath the crown of red hair that stuck out everywhere like a bright wool tassel, his eyes were smudges and his usual smile replaced by yawns. He had watched the eggs all night and was waiting to give Mia his final report on the night's watch before going to bed.

"Everything all right, Roberto?" Mia asked. She was a pleasant-faced girl with rosy cheeks and a sprinkling of cinnamon-colored freckles on her turned-up nose.

"Aye. It was all very quiet," Roberto said through a yawn. He finished the last sip of his tea.

Mia chuckled at the sleepy boy. "Good. Go on to sleep, then, and I'll see you tomorrow bright and early."

Roberto gave a weary wave of his hand and shuffled off to his bed.

"Mariko, you will have this Sun's Rising, and I will take the Sun's Falling. There may be a class of little ones coming in to observe you. Are you ready to answer their questions, or would you like my help?"

"No, I think I can do it alone," Mariko said. "I remember *my* first time in here. So many questions. I think I made the poor apprentice on duty very tired!"

"You must keep a sharp eye on the eggs, though," Mia warned. "The little ones always want to hold them."

"*Hai,* I'll watch," Mariko nodded as she set her mug down. She went to the eggs, resting in their communal nest, and touched each one lightly in greeting.

"I know, I know," said Janet, grinning as Mia

turned to face her. "I've got Night's Gathering."

"Best sleep now if you can," suggested Mia. "The night is long and it's easy to fall asleep, especially when you don't want to."

"I'll be all right," Janet answered. She finished her tea and set the mug back on the tray.

"Sleep today," repeated Mia more firmly.

"Aye, I will."

"Away, then, to your bed," Mia said, nudging Janet gently toward the door of the apprentices' sleeping rooms.

"But I just got up!" Janet protested. "Really, Mia, I promise I will sleep. A little later today. I can't right now."

Mia gazed at her, as though wanting to say more. "Well, you know yourself best," she said at last, putting her mug down next to the others. Then she went to help Mariko stoke the fires that heated the water into steam and kept the Incubation Room warm and moist.

The day passed quickly, and even when Janet found time to lie down she just couldn't sleep with all the day's noises rousing her curiosity. After she had gotten up to see a wagon with a broken wheel, children playing a clapping game, and a boy practicing a duet with his nestfriend, she began to wonder why she hadn't noticed how busy and noisy the farm was before. Or did she notice it now because she was trying so hard not to? This thought made her giggle and then sigh. She tried to imagine staying awake all night and wondered if she would get sleepy. But lying in her bed, completely awake, it was hard to think that she would ever be tired enough to sleep. Mariko and Roberto had managed. She would too.

That night in the Incubation Room, Janet wished she had slept. Her eyes were scratchy, and she caught herself at the start of a yawn.

Mia stopped by to make certain that all was well with the change of watch. "Remember," she said to Janet, "if you have any problems, even if it's the problem of staying awake, ask for help. That's why I'm here."

"Don't worry about me," Janet said, louder than she meant to. "I can do this."

"Of course you can," Mia replied gently. "But I want you to know that you are not alone. We depend on each other, and there is no shame in asking for help."

"Thank you," Janet said more humbly. "I'll remember."

When Mia left, Janet began her night duties. She noticed that the supply of wood for the fire was low. She decided to wait until later to get more from the woodpile outside. The cool bracing air would be just what she needed to revive her tired spirits in a few hours. Janet checked the water slowly simmering in the cauldron, making sure there were two full buckets beside the hearth for later. Janet fed a small eucalyptus branch into the fire and inhaled the pungent steam as it rose with a soft gray whisper. She loved the spicy smell, and it cleared her head of its drowsiness.

Then Janet went to look at the eggs in a circle in the nesting bed. She knew each egg by its shape and color. In comparison with their large dinosaur mothers, the eggs were tiny. Fatherfast had explained that if the eggs were too large, the shell would be too thick for air to go through its walls. And though small and squeaky at birth, the hatchlings grew quickly. It was one of the mysteries of life, Janet thought, that such huge and magnificent creatures came from such small beginnings.

In the history of Dinotopia it was told that once many eggs had been hatched to a single mother. But over time, the environmental limits of the island had changed the dinosaurs. Far fewer eggs were laid, and fewer still hatched. The dinosaurs came to the Hatcheries, not only to entrust the care of their eggs into the hands of humans, but also so that each generation of humans and dinosaurs could bond together from birth and strengthen their communities into one united whole.

Janet grinned thinking of the time she and Zephyr had first "fallen out of the nest," as her father said. When both she and Zephyr were very little, they had scampered into a linen closet during a game of Hide the Egg. They fell asleep while waiting to be discovered. The closet was opened and closed many times, but Janet and Zephyr were well hidden behind the sheets. Finally Zephyr made a sudden turn in her sleep, knocking open the door, and they tumbled out. Janet cried when her parents tried to put her to bed, until Zephyr came and made her own bed nearby. From that moment on, they had been inseparable.

Janet smiled at the eggs, wondering about their futures. She ran her fingers over the pebbly surface of each egg and tilted her head to listen for small sounds. But the eggs were quiet. Probably sleeping, she thought, still tiny enough to float in their watery sacs. She paid special attention to the smallest egg in the nest. The mother was Grass Sweeper, a huge Maiasaura and the nestfriend of Janet's mother. This egg had been long awaited, and both Emer and Grass Sweeper sang the song of a mother's joy at its laying.

The older dinosaurs usually produced eggs that were very delicate. So it was with Grass Sweeper. Though she was a large and sturdy dinosaur, her egg was small and fragile. Fatherfast had cautioned the apprentices about this egg in particular; it needed more attention, he told them, as its shell was much thinner. The egg glowed a pale cream color in the light of the torches, reminding Janet of a teacup she had once found washed up on the beach. She touched the egg gently with one finger and whispered a greeting.

"Janet?" Zephyr called from the doorway. "May I enter?"

"Come in, come in," Janet called.

Zephyr sat beside Janet and held her hand. "Zephyr has come to keep day in your eyes. Help to forget night."

Janet's sleepy spirits perked up. "Shall we play a game?"

"Yes. What about Put, Take, All or Nothing?" Zephyr suggested, holding up a little drawstring bag. She shook it, and Janet could hear the rattle of the four-sided top and stones used in the game.

"Hmm," she replied. "Maybe a riddling game instead. It's hard for me to do sums when I'm tired." Actually, Janet was concerned about the safety of the eggs, as Zephyr's tail tended to thrash when she got excited while playing with the numbers top.

Zephyr was disappointed, but then the sunspots over her eyes brightened again. "Oh, one I have. Out of the egg and here it is!" she squeaked excitedly.

"Give it," Janet replied, and waited to hear Zephyr's riddle.

"White rocks fill the valley!"

"Into the egg and the answer is the teeth in your mouth!" Janet exclaimed. "Out of the egg and here it is!" she challenged.

"Give it," squeaked Zephyr.

"Around I went but never moved!"

"Into the egg and the answer is a garden path!"

They continued throwing out riddles to each other, trying to catch each other in a contest of words.

And then when they couldn't think of any more riddles, they started to sing. At first they sang silly songs: songs about scooping the moon out of the water with a spoon and songs about chasing your tail. These made both of them laugh. As the night wore on, their songs got slower. Finally Zephyr sang one long song about the slow changes of the seasons, and as her voice rumbled the tune of winter her head nodded sleepily.

Janet too was almost lulled into a wintry nap by Zephyr's song, but a crackle of firewood made her startle awake again. "Zephyr, go on to your bed," she said, nudging the dinosaur. "You're tired."

"Janet, nestfriend, I must stay. Give help."

"No, really, I'm all right," Janet insisted. "I can do this job by myself. You should sleep. One of us has to be cheerful tomorrow!" she said with a laugh.

Reluctantly Zephyr got up and headed for the door. "Is it certain, Janet?" she asked, turning at the door to the Incubation Room.

"Aye, go on now," Janet repeated. "Sleep for both of us."

Zephyr scratched her chin sleepily and left. In the quiet warmth of the Incubation Room, Janet sighed. Then she shook herself awake and set about her tasks once more. Carefully she brushed away the grassy bedding, rotated each egg, and tucked the bedding securely around the eggs once more. She listened to each egg, hoping to catch the tiny piping of its first song. She refilled the water in the cauldrons and stoked the fire. Then she decided to bring in new wood from the woodpile. At the door of the Incubation Room, Janet glanced back, making sure that all was well before she ventured outside.

The night air was cool and dry. Janet looked up at the sky. The stars were like diamonds stitched into the velvety cloth of night. The moon was as round and full as an egg itself. Janet breathed in the night air, enjoying the rich grassy scent of the farm. She stretched her limbs, the blood tingling in her fingertips.

"Come on, Janet," she urged herself. "Stay awake!"

As Janet made her way to the shadowy woodpile she heard a strange noise. She stopped to listen. It was a jingling, and then someone shouting out numbers. Janet followed the sound, which became louder as she walked the length of the Hatchery building.

She peeked around the corner of the building and smiled. A troupe of performers had camped in the field beside the farm and were rehearsing their show. The firelight played over a man and a woman in costumes of wildly colored patches. The man wore a mask with a large funny nose that covered half of his face. At the end of the nose was a bell that jingled when he shook his head. The woman wore a red, green, and yellow hat with three points with more bells on them.

The couple were throwing small clubs and balls and plates to each other, shouting out a number each time an object was added to the toss. Janet watched, dazzled by the array of flying objects. Then they began to neatly catch each object. One by one everything was set down until nothing was left in the air. The jugglers turned to an imaginary audience, arms outstretched, and bowed.

Janet applauded. The performers looked up, surprised to see her. The man grinned widely beneath the huge nose and motioned for Janet to sit on the grass.

"Come, come," he invited. "A rehearsal always goes better with an appreciative audience."

"Well, just for a moment," Janet said. "I really must get back."

"As long as you may," the woman said, bobbing into a curtsy, and the bells on her three-pointed hat jingled merrily.

Janet sat down in the long grass and told herself it would be for only one moment—just long enough to see the next act. But once the actors began, she forgot about the time. The man and the woman were joined by their companion dinosaurs. The two Hypsilophodons juggled flaming torches on their heads and tails, creating a bridge of firelight. Beneath the arc the man and the woman tossed little buckets, which spilled tiny scraps of paper like water droplets.

Next the man balanced spinning plates on the tips of long poles. He rested his pole on his masked forehead, his huge nose pointing up to the sky. Janet clapped her hands as the man then placed a long row

21

of poles and spinning plates down the bony spine of an Ankylosaurus.

Then the five performers began to juggle small white balls—first two, then four, then six. The balls pulsed from hand to head, to hand, and then to tail. Janet's eyelids grew heavy following the hypnotic movement, the brilliant white flashes like shooting stars between the performers. Without knowing when it happened, her head nodded and her chin drooped to her chest. Beneath her half-closed eyelids, she could just see the white flash of the balls as they passed from hand to hand.

With a whispery sigh, she stretched out on the soft grass, her limbs curling like a leaf around her. I should be somewhere, she thought dimly, struggling to rise. But the flashing balls made her so sleepy that she couldn't quite remember what she had been doing before. It's all right, she told herself, settling into the earth. In the morning. That's when she'd remember what she was supposed to do.

Janet dreamed she was wearing a brightly patched costume. She was throwing balls to Zephyr, who caught them neatly on her tail. She frowned in her sleep as the balls suddenly turned into eggs and one slipped between her fingers. Then the dream shifted away, and Janet thought no more about it.

Janet awoke when someone shook her shoulder. The dew was wet on her face, and she could smell the cool earth.

"Janet! Oh, Janet, is it well with you?" Zephyr called.

"Zephyr," Janet groaned, turning sleepily on the grass. She squinted up into the bright sunlight. "Why are you waking me so early?" Janet mumbled.

"The eggs, Janet nestfriend," Zephyr replied, her voice squeaking higher with worry.

"Eggs," Janet repeated. Then the cold splash of memory woke her. "Oh, no!" she cried, sitting up quickly. "I fell asleep watching the jugglers! Oh, I hope everything is all right!"

Janet scrambled to her feet and ran with Zephyr to the Incubation Room. She entered the room, then stopped when she saw Roberto and Fatherfast huddled over the nest of eggs. The room was cool and very dry. The water had boiled away, and the fire had died down.

"Are they all right?" Janet asked, hurrying to the nest.

Fatherfast leaned up from the nest at the sound of her voice and turned to face her. His crimson crest was a pale mud color. Janet felt the breath catch in her throat at the sight of Roberto's grave expression. He held an egg close to his chest wrapped in damp moss. Janet recognized it as Grass Sweeper's egg.

"Is it well with you, Janet?" Fatherfast asked slowly. "You are not hurt?"

"No, Fatherfast, I am well enough."

"How is it you left your post?"

"I...I got distracted."

"By what, then?"

Janet felt horrible. She didn't want to say the words. Her cheeks flamed red with embarrassment. She looked up into Fatherfast's patient gaze and knew she had no choice. She had to give him an answer.

"I watched some actors, Fatherfast, rehearsing in the field. I fell asleep on the grass. I didn't mean to," she said quickly.

"I am certain of that," Fatherfast replied softly, but Janet was sure she heard disappointment in his voice. She had neglected her duty to the eggs.

"Are they all right?" Janet asked.

"All but one. Grass Sweeper's egg has a small crack. Perhaps it is nothing. Perhaps it was always there, but the change in the moisture and the heat of the air has made us aware of it. Special care must now be taken to be sure of its successful hatching."

"I'm so sorry. I really didn't mean...I promise I won't..." Janet said, trying desperately to find the words to apologize, to put everything back as it had been before. But that was impossible.

Emer appeared at the doorway of the Incubation Room. The morning sun glinted off her glasses, and her mouth was set in a worried frown. In the resting chamber, Janet could hear Grass Sweeper singing a song to her egg, and her eyes filled with tears.

"Are you happy that all is well?" Zephyr asked, softly nudging Janet as the tears made their way down her cheeks.

"No. I'm miserable because I was so stupid and may have injured Grass Sweeper's egg."

"Don't worry, Janet. All will be well," Zephyr said to comfort her.

Roberto had finished wrapping the fragile egg in moss. Mia took the egg into a small room off the main Incubation Room, where it would remain covered with damp moss and half buried in a deep bed of warmed sand.

"All will be well again," Fatherfast said. He touched her lightly on the shoulder. "But, Janet, you must go and collect your thoughts. Think and learn from this. Even a mistake well examined is useful."

"But who will take my watch with the eggs?"

"Mia will for now. Give yourself time to rest and think," Fatherfast answered.

Janet left the Incubation Room, treading slowly up the stairs to the sleeping quarters. Roberto reached out to pat her on the shoulder, but she shrugged him off. She was too angry with herself and too worried at the thought of Grass Sweeper's egg being hurt because of her stupidity. When Zephyr joined her on the stairs, Janet stopped her.

"I need to be alone," Janet said.

Zephyr's golden eyes gazed down, the sunspots fading over her brows. "As you want. But always am I here to listen, Janet."

"I just need to be alone," Janet said more firmly. She didn't want anyone to be nice to her. She felt awful, and there wasn't anybody who could change that. She wanted to crawl under the bed and stay there forever.

Zephyr gave a mournful sigh. Janet went wearily to her room, only the sound of Grass Sweeper's sad song following after her.

CHAPTER 3

Janet lay on her bed and listened to the sounds of the Hatchery. She knew that by the midday meal every-one—from the smallest child to the biggest dinosaur on the farm—would have heard about her failure. And if anything happened to the egg...Janet groaned and turned restlessly in her bed. She couldn't think about Grass Sweeper; it made her feel too guilty. How could she ever face Grass Sweeper again if something happened to her egg?

In the evening her father, Stefano, brought her a bowl of soup and some bread. He set the meal on a small table.

"You missed your supper," he said.

"Thanks, but I'm not hungry," Janet answered, sitting up in the bed.

"Come, Janet, let us talk," said her father, putting his hand gently on her shoulder.

"I can't yet," she said, staring down into her lap.

"No one is angry at you."

"*I'm* angry at me," she whispered.

"All the more reason to join us. Talk, and feel at peace with yourself again."

Janet remained silent, because she knew if she spoke, she would cry. She wanted to join her parents and the others, but she couldn't yet.

"Eat some soup, then," her father prodded. "It might help you feel better."

Janet looked up at her father's kind face. He had dark curly hair like hers, though now it was starting to gray. His eyes were a warm brown. Beneath the full fringe of his graying mustache he gave a slight smile. The soup steamed with a fragrant smell, and Janet realized that she was indeed hungry. But it felt as though a stone were stuck in her throat, and she couldn't bring herself to pick up the spoon.

"I can't eat, Da," Janet whispered. "I just keep thinking that I can't be a Hatchery apprentice anymore. It's too dangerous. I'm not trustworthy."

"Janet, you're much too hard on yourself," Stefano protested. "You are not the first apprentice to fall asleep on the watch, I can assure you of that."

"But Grass Sweeper's egg…what if I have harmed it?" Janet asked, blinking as tears filled her eyes.

"Fatherfast will see to the egg's care. It will be all right. Listen, Janet," her father said. "Everyone has to learn their job, and everyone makes mistakes. No one is born perfect—even a shell may have flaws. Come down now and be with us. Let us help you."

"Later," Janet said. "I still need to think."

"Fair enough. Think, my daughter, but don't punish yourself too much," he added.

He left Janet alone again, with the soup cooling on the table beside the bed. Janet chewed her fingernails and thought about what her father had said, but she still couldn't forgive herself. Now she knew she was a terrible Hatchery apprentice—the only thing she had ever wanted to be. She couldn't even do a simple but important task such as staying awake on her shift. How many more eggs might she endanger if she stayed? Deep down, Janet knew she was also afraid to face everyone on the farm. She shuddered; what an awful mess she had made of things!

Janet tried to gather her courage to go downstairs, to face them all. She could hear the talking and laughter. But she couldn't seem to move her feet beyond the top of the stairs. She had built a wall around herself, and she didn't know how to break it. So she stayed alone, wishing that she could go back in time and do the shift over again. The right way.

Finally as darkness settled and the farm grew quiet, Janet made up her mind.

"I'll run away," she said aloud. "I'll go to the city and find work. But I won't be a Hatchery hand. I won't be a danger to another egg, ever again." And I won't have to face the others either, she thought.

Janet gathered a few belongings in a small satchel. She drank the cold soup and packed the bread for later. She started to cry thinking about her family, Zephyr, and all the people and dinosaurs she would never see again. "But it's better this way," she told herself. "I failed everybody. Better I should go."

Janet threw a black cape over her shoulders and crept down the stairs to the Incubation Room. She waited by the door until Mariko's back was turned, then she slipped quietly across the room to the outside door, fresh tears welling up at the sight of the eggs. Out in the courtyard she stopped, letting the tears cool on her cheeks. She turned to look back at the farm, noting that the light in her parents' room still burned. She could go to them, she thought. No, she decided, she had disappointed them too.

Suddenly something ran into her. She stifled a scream as a face loomed up and hands clasped her shoulders. By moonlight Janet saw Zephyr's eyes shining a bright silver.

"Zephyr! You scared me! What are you doing here?"

"Janet, nestfriend," squeaked Zephyr, "what is it you are doing here? Zephyr waits all day, hoping that you will come to her. Hoping that together we will sing a song of harmony again. Sadness, like work and joy, must be shared."

"Oh, Zephyr, I'm so sorry," Janet whispered.

"Is it angry you are with Zephyr?"

"Angry?" Janet asked, confused. "Why should I be angry with you?"

"Think of others before self. That is our rule. But

I didn't. I left you, and sleep came to take my place. I should have helped you through the Night's Gathering."

Janet hugged Zephyr around her slender neck. "No, Zephyr. It wasn't your fault. It wasn't your job to stay awake. It was mine. And I failed. So I am running away. The Hatchery will be better off without a mindsinging, daydreaming girl like me."

"No, Janet, not true at all. Families will worry. Mother and father will cry. Don't despairing be. Grass Sweeper will not speak ill. You are not bad, Janet. Stay. Stay with Zephyr. I will talk with Fatherfast." Zephyr's tail waved anxiously as she spoke.

"No!" Janet said firmly. "You spoke for me once, Zephyr. I can't let you speak for me again."

"Janet, you are stone hitting stone. Give instead."

"I'm going," Janet said. "My mind is made up."

"Then I, too, am coming," Zephyr said. "We are nestfriends. Together it must be."

"Do you mean that?" Janet asked, relieved that she would not face the unknown road alone.

"We will travel together, help each other, and—"

"And what?" Janet asked as Zephyr paused and scratched herself along her neck.

"And come home together, Janet. Here to the Hatchery. Later?" she added hopefully.

"I won't come back," Janet insisted.

"Perhaps," Zephyr squeaked in a small voice. "But for now you may ride on my back through this night. Then we will see what sings with the sun's hatching."

"Won't I be too heavy for you?" Janet asked.

"You are yet a hatchling, and I can carry you still. Come, let us go," Zephyr answered.

Zephyr inclined her neck, straightening her back to make it easier for Janet to scramble up. Janet clapped her thighs against Zephyr's sides as the dinosaur moved quickly and with a fast, bouncy gait.

"Ready?" Zephyr asked.

Janet took one more look over her shoulder at the moon rising high above the Hatchery. Then she looked back to where the open road disappeared into the tall waving grass of the fields. She wrapped her arms around Zephyr's neck.

"Ready!" she answered.

And then Zephyr began to run, her powerful legs stretching out, her clawed feet digging into the mud of the road and casting little clods of freed dirt behind her. With her head lowered for speed, Zephyr's body lengthened into a long slender shadow over the road, spangled now and again by moonlight glancing off her scales. Janet held on, her head tucked into Zephyr's neck to keep the rushing wind out of her face. A sailor's dream, her father once said of the speeding dinosaur. Not a creature of muscle and bone, but a wind let loose over the land.

Janet sighed into the cool gushing air that smelled of damp soil and new grass. She was leaving the terrible sense of failure and disappointment behind. She would turn herself to a new direction and start over as someone else. No one would know what a dismal job she had made of her apprenticeship. She thought of how her parents would miss her. The memory of them clutched her, made the tears smart in her eyes once more. Quickly, she put the thought away, not wanting anything to change her mind.

Zephyr ran through the night. The road curved into a quiet wood, and ginkgoes and pines made a soft canopy of branches over their heads. Silvery stars winked at them from between the rustling leaves. Finally Zephyr slowed her pace to a walk. Janet loosened her grip and leaned wearily against the dinosaur. The slow, rocking gait of Zephyr's walk began to lull Janet to sleep, and she could feel the dinosaur's fatigue.

"Stop, Zephyr," Janet mumbled. "I am too heavy. And I can't keep my eyes open."

"Falling off you are," Zephyr teased, but Janet could hear the relief in her nestfriend's voice.

Zephyr stopped, and Janet slid down from her back. Her legs trembled from the effort of holding on to Zephyr's back for so long.

"Where, nestfriend?" Zephyr asked, looking into the shadows of the forest.

"Oh, anywhere," groaned Janet wearily. She wrapped her cape around her and lay down beneath the spreading leaves of a nearby fern patch. She could hear Zephyr circling in the ferns, scratching at the soil as she prepared a shallow nest. Finally, Zephyr gave a low whistle and sank to the ground next to Janet. Leaves brushed lightly against Janet's face, tickling her cheek. Then a soft tearing and clicking noise started.

"Zephyr, are you eating my bed?" Janet mumbled.

The clicking noise stopped.

"Just a little. There is hunger in me, and your bed is very tender."

Janet chuckled and tucked her chin deeper into the cape. "Just leave me a bit of pillow," she murmured.

If Zephyr answered her, Janet didn't hear; within the muffled folds of her cape, she found a deep quiet of sleep and dreams.

She dreamed of watching her bare feet making muddy prints as she ran. Her arms ached from carrying a heavy burden. She wanted to set it down and free her aching arms, but she couldn't. Whatever she held remained in her arms. She looked down and saw that she held an egg, wrapped in a bed of green moss. She groaned in her sleep. She could run, run forever, but the responsibility would always be with her, always in her arms.

Janet awoke, her hands clenched in fists. She stared at the night sky, confused for a moment by the stars twinkling between the leaves. Then she remembered that she was running away from home. She closed her eyes again and curled closer to Zephyr.

CHAPTER 4

Rain spattered through the branches of the trees onto the leaves of the ferns and then trickled onto Janet's upturned face. She moaned and sat up. Her cape was soaked and her body chilled from sleeping on the ground. The light was dim, the sun hidden behind a thick bank of rain clouds.

Zephyr lay beside her, half buried in the soft soil, her nose tucked beneath her forearms, her tail curled close to her body. Her color was pale, as though the cold rain had washed away its brightness. She looked like a huge stone, gray and quiet amid the brilliant green of the ferns.

"Zephyr!" Janet called, afraid for her nestfriend. Janet had never seen Zephyr so still. Zephyr's scales had always flickered, even when she was sleeping. But now she was quiet and motionless.

Slowly, Zephyr opened her eyes and raised her head. She moved stiffly. "Cold, Janet," she rasped. Her eyes were the color of faded cornstalks.

"And wet," answered Janet, shivering in her

drenched cape. She looked up at the canopy of trees, the rain pattering down on them. A gust of wind shook a pine branch and scattered rain in her face. "Do you know where we are, Zephyr?" she asked.

"No. Only where we were going. But not there yet."

"I think we should get moving again. We need to find some shelter from this rain."

"Home?" Zephyr asked hopefully.

"No," Janet said with determination. "Not home. I want to go on, to Cornucopia."

Janet stood up and shook out the small leaves and twigs that clung to her drenched shawl. She stamped her feet to bring warmth back into her limbs.

"Come on, Zephyr. Maybe there is a farm or a cottage farther up the road. There must be other people traveling, even in this rain. Maybe there will be someone to help us."

Zephyr nodded, though Janet could read her disappointment in the drooping tail. "Come then, Janet. On my back."

"Are you sure? I know I'm heavy to carry."

"If I carry you it will be faster, so sooner we will find shelter and maybe warmth. "

"All right," Janet agreed, and climbed up on Zephyr's back. "But promise you will tell me when I am too much to carry."

"Promised it is," answered Zephyr. She lowered her head and began to trot lightly through the rain.

Her feet squelched in the muddy road, leaving deep prints that filled with rainwater, forming a trail of tiny lakes behind them.

They traveled throughout the day, stopping beneath the broad branches of a pine tree when the rain fell in fists of water. Janet was soaked through with rain and spattered with mud. Her cape hung heavy on her shoulders. She was hungry and very cold. Zephyr was quiet, her scales a pale color. Her tail drooped into the mud when they walked side by side on the road. But still they traveled, Janet's eyes trained forward up the road for the sight of a cottage or a farm.

The road seemed to go on forever through the dense forest of pine, cedar, and ginkgo trees. As the day darkened with the approach of night Janet began to give up hope. Then she saw a strange gold light flicker at the corner of her vision. She stopped and turned to look for it. Over the earthy scent of the forest, she caught the peppery aroma of wood smoke. A farm, she thought. Or maybe the campfire of another traveler. The gold light winked in and out between the dark, wet tree trunks.

"There!" she said excitedly to Zephyr. "Up there a ways in the forest. There must be a cottage. Let's go!"

"Janet, it is away from the road," Zephyr said. "We may get lost."

"We have to find it, Zephyr. It's too cold to stay out here," Janet argued.

"I am with you, nestfriend," Zephyr sighed. "Better it is to find warmth."

They followed a narrow mud trail through a thick carpet of ferns and tangled bushes. It seemed to Janet that they walked for a long time, never reaching the light. Farther and farther from the road they went, the gold light dancing in and out between the dark branches as they struggled to reach it. Finally Zephyr burst through a heavy thicket, and they found themselves standing in the front garden of a lopsided cottage.

Compared to the huge buildings of the Hatchery, the cottage appeared small to Janet. It squatted, fat and hunched-shouldered, beneath the trees. The whole cottage leaned to one side, the door not square on its hinges. The thatched roof was a dark gray, except where moss grew in bright green clumps around the eaves. Beneath the front door was a large gap where firelight seeped out over the stones of the stoop. Over the door were painted two eyes, slanting upward, the pupils a bright spot of white in the dark gray afternoon. They seemed to stare down at Janet with curiosity.

Zephyr and Janet picked their way carefully through planted rows of vegetables and soggy flowers. At the door Janet hesitated, suddenly shy to knock, despite the cold. Then the rumble of thunder urged her forward to the door, as did the promise of a fire and a dry place in which to stop.

Janet knocked and then waited. When there was no answer she put her ear to the door. She could hear someone singing inside. She rapped her knuckles harder against the battered door and heard the distant thunder echo the sound of her knocking. The singing stopped abruptly, and in the near quiet Janet knocked once more and called out.

"Hallo? Is there anyone within?"

The door opened with a furious creak, as though the hinges were angry at being made to move on such a cold, wet day. An old woman with short white hair capping a face as brown as an acorn peered out in surprise at the sight of Janet and Zephyr at her door. Then she grinned widely, her smile showing a few gaps where her teeth were missing.

"A la!" she exclaimed, throwing open the door. The dry heat of the cottage reached them like a warm summer breeze. *"Maskini! Maskini! Karibu, watoto wangu!* Come in, poor things, come in," she said, plucking Janet by a wet sleeve. "How wet you are, my children!" she tsked, and drew Janet and Zephyr to the fire inside. She took a bright-colored cloth hanging on the wall and held it up for Janet. "Take off your wet clothes, and wrap in this."

"Thank you, but I am fine," Janet lied. "Just a moment by your fire is all I need."

The woman laughed, a generous sound which filled the cottage. In the rafters a family of alphadons tittered and squeaked. They peered down, their eyes gleaming a bright gold. The father held a reed flute in his hands. The mother hung upside down from a long coiling tail. Babies clung to the silvery fur of her back, chattering noisily.

"Stay, stay," they cried out in a chorus. "Sada is here to help the weary stranger, the one lost from the path, strayed into the woods."

Janet looked again at the older woman holding out the dry cloth. She was slim, not much taller than Janet, but with strong arms. Though she was simply dressed, she looked elegant in her white cotton tunic with gold and black embroidery. Her feet were bare, and a gold bracelet circled one small ankle.

"Come," she repeated, shaking out the cloth in her hands.

"Well, I guess I should," Janet answered. She shivered as she wriggled free of her soaked jacket and shirt. Water dribbled out of her boots, and she peeled off her wet trousers. Sada wrapped the thick cloth around Janet's body, tucking the end in at her armpit. She gave Janet a second cloth, smelling of sandalwood, which Janet used to dry her hair and then wrapped around her bare shoulders.

Zephyr crooned softly all the while, turning around slowly as she basked in the warm glow of the fire. Her scales glittered and sparkled, and the gold and blue color returned to her face.

Sada hung Janet's clothes on hooks before the fire. Steam curled from the wet cloth and clung to the windows. Sada bustled to a long table and laid out bowls of food. She set two candles down and lit them.

"Come and eat," she invited Janet and Zephyr.

Janet's stomach began to growl at the sight of food. She threw herself down on a bench and began to eat. Next to her, Zephyr balanced her tail over the edge of the bench and, chuckling happily, rolled long green plants between her palms, releasing their sweet scent before she nibbled them. Janet ate bread and dried fruit and a warm porridge soup. She had a plate of bright orange sweet potatoes and white roasted cassavas. Sada watched Janet and Zephyr eat, her elbows propped on the table as she rested her chin on her hands. The alphadons came down from the rafters, and the father played a tune on his flute.

"Where are you from? What's your name? How did you come here?" chorused the young alphadons, their small faces eagerly staring up at Janet and then Zephyr.

"Have you come from far away?" one asked.

"Does your mama know you're here?" asked another.

"Aye and no," answered Janet quickly between bites.

"And which is which?" Sada asked, her head leaning forward. Janet looked up from her plate and was caught by the keen gaze of Sada's brown eyes.

"I mean, I've come from far away," Janet said.

"And does your mother know that you have come

to this wood?" Sada asked quietly.

"No," Janet said.

"Ah." Sada leaned back and crossed her arms. She said nothing but pursed her lips together as she studied first Janet and then Zephyr. Zephyr glanced at Janet, a spark lighting her yellow eyes.

"I left the Hatchery in a hurry. I didn't have time to tell anyone," Janet fumbled for words that wouldn't give her away.

"The Hatchery," Sada echoed, her white eyebrows lifted in surprise.

"Aye."

"A la, but you have journeyed a long way. It is no wonder you are wet and hungry," Sada replied. "And what business takes you this far from home?"

"This food is wonderful, and I really must thank you for being so kind to us," Janet said quickly, changing the direction of the conversation.

"But that is why I am here," Sada chuckled. "All find their way to me in times of need."

"Really? How?" Janet asked, confused.

Sada gave her deep throaty laugh again. "I came here in time past, maybe as you come here now," she added, pointing to Janet. "In too much of a hurry to tell anyone. But I looked to be alone, and so I was. Then one day someone came that needed me. And then another and another. Seasons have come and gone, but always there is someone knocking at my door. I know I am here for a reason. To be of help."

"Where are you from?" Janet asked, reaching for a mango.

"Waterfall City," Sada answered. Her eyes misted as she looked away into the fire where the steam still curled up from Janet's wet clothes.

"Oh, how wonderful!" Janet cried. "I've always wanted to go there. Were you born there?"

Sada nodded. "*Ndio,* yes. I am five mothers Swahili. My family were traders, traveling once on the ocean in blue-and-white sailboats they called dhows. On the boat were painted eyes with which to see the world." Then Sada chuckled. "Though I do not think my people had Dinotopia in their thoughts."

"There are eyes over your door now," Zephyr said.

"*Ndio.* I keep them there to look out for the one in need."

"But why did you leave Waterfall City?" Janet asked, intrigued.

Sada shrugged. "Things were said and done in haste. By the time I understood what I had done, I had come too far and could not turn back."

"Were you not forgiven?" Janet asked, her fingers curling into a worried fist in her lap.

Sada stood and crossed to the fire. She bent down and fed another log into the blazing coals. In the firelight her skin was a copper color. She turned to Janet and smiled.

"I could have returned, but I chose differently."

"Do you wish you had gone back?"

Sada gave a sad smile. "Sometimes. There are days when I wonder how it might have been. But the years have passed and my life is here. And what about you? There is still time. Perhaps you will not have to wonder what sadness your leaving caused."

Janet was quiet, and Zephyr watched her hopefully. Doubt tapped on her heart, forcing Janet to think hard about what she was doing. It was all so complicated, hard to face her family at the farm. But equally hard to leave the life she loved. Tears formed in Janet's eyes.

"Ah, too much sorrow," Sada said quickly. "We have water enough from the rain. Dry your tears and we will talk of other things. For one, you have not told us your names."

Janet wiped her eyes with the back of her hand and gave a thin smile. "I am Janet Morgan. And this is my nestfriend, Zephyr."

"It is well to see you at our table," Sada said. "Is there anything else you would like? Some tea?"

Janet sighed. "That would be wonderful."

Sada chuckled and brought out glasses and a copper teapot. She put a big pinch of green leaves into the teapot and added boiling water from the hearth. A fragrant scent of mint filled the room as the tea steeped.

Zephyr scratched her neck and crooned. "The grass is sweet. My neck is warm. May this one sing thanks?" she asked, sunspots flashing over her eyes.

Sada beamed and clapped. "Songs are good. Come.

Bring your chairs by the fire and we will join you."

Janet got up from the table and moved two chairs, one for Sada and one for herself, near the little stone hearth of the fireplace. Zephyr sat on her haunches on a rug woven of dried rushes. The alphadons scrambled off the table and seated themselves alongside the hearth on a low bench. Their silver-tipped fur gleamed in the firelight.

Sada set the tea glasses down on the hearth. She took down a hollow gourd with narrow prongs attached at one end. Sada held the gourd in her lap and ran her thumbs over the prongs. They made a soft rippling noise.

"What is that instrument?" Janet asked.

"It's a marimba," Sada said, smiling, "and it always brings joy. Listen and you will see." Sada played her thumb over the marimba in a swift complex rhythm. Inside the gourd the notes resonated with a sweet hollow sound, soft as the rain falling on the thatch. The father alphadon put his reed flute to his mouth and began to add a second melody that soared over the marimba's voice. The babies scampered off the benches and gathered up seed-filled rattles, which they shook in time to the music.

Janet had never heard such music before. Zephyr's eyes glowed with curiosity and then excitement as she listened, waiting for the right moment to add her voice to the growing music. When Zephyr began to sing, her voice made a soft huffing sound, like palms

45

brushing over a drum; gentle and quiet as she impro-
vised with the unfamiliar music. Slowly she grew more
confident and added her own melody. It blended with
the high reedy voice of the pipes and the low rippling
of Sada's marimba. Zephyr's voice wove into the others' music so smoothly, it was if she had grown up
singing with them.

"How did you do that?" Janet asked Zephyr when
the music stopped.

"Zephyr listens. Hears what is in the heart," she
answered simply.

"I could never do that," Janet said sadly.

"Of course you can," Sada said, sitting down next
to her. "As can everyone in their own way. Zephyr
hears the heart in music. But you, Janet, perhaps your
skill lies elsewhere."

"I don't know," Janet said. "I seem to make a mess
of everything."

"I have never seen the Hatcheries, though I read
about them in Waterfall City," Sada said, as she
cracked a nut on the table. "Tell me about them." She
handed Janet a piece of the nut. "Are they as beautiful
and tranquil as they say?"

"Oh, aye," Janet answered. "Our farm is beautiful.
The buildings are large but very comfortable."

"Bigger than my cottage?" Sada said with a grin.

"Oh, much bigger. There is plenty of space for the
dinosaurs and the three human families that live at
the farm. Then there are apprentices from other farms

and the Hatchery building itself."

"And who built such wonders?" Sada asked.

"Many hands," Zephyr said. "Together."

"And the dinosaurs?" Sada prodded.

"Oh, there are many generations that have come to our Hatchery. Fatherfast, the Ovinutrix who serves the farm as our teacher, is famous. There is nothing about the hatching of eggs that he doesn't know. I've learned a great deal from him."

"Ah, you are very lucky to be near such wisdom," Sada nodded. "And what is the life like there?"

Janet's face glowed in the firelight. "In the cool season, when the grass is at its sweetest, we harvest the hay. Everyone is in the fields, and there are singing competitions to keep the harvesters moving quickly. It's the only time we are free from nursery school work, and even though it's hard, I love it."

"And tasty," Zephyr sighed in her throat.

"Then, in the warm season, our studies are hard. We learn from all the dinosaurs who come to us for their hatching as well as the regular history and hatchery lessons. There is much to do, but every day brings something new to learn."

"Ah, you are a good student, then. Not afraid of the work," Sada said.

The wood crackled in the fireplace as Janet's mind turned. It was true. She *was* a good student, loving the learning even when it was difficult. And though she was a daydreamer sometimes, she always did her best.

Suddenly Janet realized how much she was going to miss her classes and the hard but satisfying work of the farm.

"Tell me about hatchings. I have always wanted to see such a wonder," Sada said quietly.

"It is a miracle," Janet said softly, staring into the fire. "The shell is rough, but the hatchling picks at it for hours, slowly freeing itself. We do not interfere, helping only if needed. Dinosaurs gather around the Hatchery and sing songs of welcome. Hatching is just the first of many important journeys in a dinosaur's life. Finally the hatchling frees himself from the shell, and there is quiet as he sings his first song."

Janet fell silent, remembering. The memories filled her heart, making it hard for her to speak.

Sada squeezed Janet's hand. "You must go home. There is nothing to compare with what you have left."

"I can't. I made a stupid mistake."

"You are forgiven already. Go home where you are loved and needed. You must face your mistake. Learn from it, and later this season you will be there to see the new hatchlings. It is the right thing to do."

Janet looked up into Sada's deep brown eyes. "Are you sure?"

"Absolutely. It will be hard. But I can see it is the right road for you. Do not abandon your dream."

"But what about you, Sada? You left Waterfall City and found a life here. Why couldn't I do the same?"

Sada shook her head. "La, *mtoto wangu*, no, my child. This was my dream. To come here to this far distant place. I didn't want to live in the city. It made my family sad, but they understood. You are a Hatchery child and you love it. So you must go home, or you will always be unhappy and lonely."

Janet gave a huge sigh, the weight of homesickness leaving her as she felt her mind change. "I'll go home. I'll face them, and I'll work even harder than before."

Sada gave Janet's hands another squeeze. "*Nzuri. Nzuri sana.* Very good. You are a brave girl."

Zephyr patted her hands together and scratched her neck with pleasure. "Home, nestfriend. We will go home together."

Janet grinned at the bright flashing sunspots over Zephyr's eyes. Then she yawned, exhausted from the long journey in the rain.

Sada set out a mattress of rushes, covering it with a linen sheet and a brightly woven blanket. "Come, here is your nest," she said, giving Janet a little pillow that smelled like a field of flowers.

Janet and Zephyr lay down on the mattress with their backs rubbing against each other. Janet imagined herself home, hugging her mother and father and greeting everyone she knew. She would make it up to them all. She would work hard and make sure that Grass Sweeper's egg hatched.

Sada blew out the candles, but the firelight continued to flicker over the walls of the cottage. She played her marimba lightly, the soft music joining with the sound of the falling rain. Janet fell into a peaceful sleep and dreamed of the Hatchery.

CHAPTER 5

The cottage was quiet and still when Janet awoke. She rose and looked out the small window. She saw the forest shrouded with a veil of pearl gray fog so thick she could barely see the spindly plants in Sada's garden. Beyond the rim of the garden the forest was a solid shadow of soft gray. Moisture clung to the window and dripped in tiny rivers over the sill.

"Not a good day for travel," Sada said. She had risen from her bed and was lighting the fire. "Stay a while longer, at least until the mist has lifted," she urged, blowing on the coals.

"Oh, we'll be all right," Janet said. "Once we are on the road, it will be easy to find the way."

"But my home is not near the road. And the path to it may be hidden by the fog. Are you sure you will not wait a little while longer?"

Janet turned an eager face to Sada. "Aye. I want to go home. While I still have the courage to face everybody. It won't take us long. I'm sure of it."

"Zephyr can fly over the road. Fast as wind,"

Zephyr added as she woke to their conversation. "Home to the Hatchery will I take us, Sada."

Sada crossed her arms over her chest and pursed her lips in worried thought. Then she sighed and shrugged. "*Nzuri sana.* All right. Home calls to you. But, my children, go carefully into the forest. I will give you some extra food and blankets, should your journey take longer than you planned."

Janet dressed quickly, her clothes stiff and scratchy from drying by the fire. Sada rolled a blanket, which she placed over Zephyr's neck. Then she bustled around, packing extra food into a string bag. She slung the bag over Janet's shoulder and smiled into her face. "Brave heart," she said softly, and patted Janet's cheek.

Janet wanted to thank Sada for being there when they needed her. Not only had she sheltered two strangers from the rain; she had also shared her stories and wisdom. Janet would always be grateful to Sada for giving her the courage to face her mistakes, look into her heart, and make the decision to return to the Hatchery. It seemed too huge a gift for which to thank someone.

As if she could see into Janet's mind, Sada gave a low laugh and clapped a hand on Janet's shoulder. "I am glad you and Zephyr came to brighten our lives on such a miserable night. Good journey to you, Janet, and to you, Zephyr, nestfriend."

"Thank you, Sada," Janet said, "for everything.

May I come back sometime? When I'm not in trouble?" she added with a grin.

"*Ndio,* yes, my child. You are always welcome here."

"New songs will I bring!" Zephyr squeaked.

Sada laughed and stroked the dinosaur on her neck. Zephyr glowed a bright silvery blue. "It will be a whole night of song," she promised.

They went outside together and stood shivering in the cool morning air. Janet got on Zephyr's back and waved farewell to Sada and the small lopsided cottage. As she and Zephyr wove between the mist and the trees, Janet looked over her shoulder. The mist parted for a moment, and Janet saw the bright blue painted eyes over the door staring after them. It looked as if they blinked a farewell just as the mist closed around them in a thick gray glove.

Janet and Zephyr went along slowly as they looked for the little dirt path that had led them to Sada's cottage the night before. Neither of them could remember how far off the main road they had walked. The rain had been so heavy that it was hard to recall exactly where they had traveled through the trees.

The day stayed gray and murky. Around them the fog muffled all noises except for the gentle drip of lingering raindrops seeping through the branches of the trees. Ginkgoes and conifers brushed against them, and water droplets fell on their heads when they shook the branches. All the muddy paths disappeared without warning beneath thick green ferns. Hours passed, and Janet's stomach began to grumble for a midday meal.

"There!" Janet said, finally spotting a footprint denting the red mud.

"Not mine, nestfriend," Zephyr answered.

"Isn't it? Who else could it belong to?"

"Another one travels in the woods. It is too big to be mine. This is not a foot you see, but a toe," Zephyr said, pointing to a wider area around the print.

Janet saw that the surrounding ferns had been crushed to create a wide, deep impression. She frowned, disappointed and a little worried.

"Zephyr, is there any danger from the owner of this footprint?" Janet asked.

"I'm thinking not. Looks like leaf eater. Not bone-crunching dinosaur."

"Well, that's something to be grateful for, I guess," Janet said. She sighed wearily at the mist. Perhaps Sada had been right; they should have waited for the fog to clear. If only they could find the main road!

Hoping for a sign that the fog was thinning, Janet looked up into the sky. But the clouds remained thick and gray, the sun hidden. If anything, the mist seemed even denser than before. Janet's hair had bunched into curls. Water was dripping down the back of her neck into her shirt. And she felt as if the dampness of the day had seeped into her skin and settled in her muscles for good.

Janet shivered. "Zephyr, are we lost?"

"No," Zephyr said, shaking her head. Water droplets scattered from her scales.

"Then where are we?"

"In the woods."

"But where in the woods? And where is the main road?"

"Ah," said Zephyr with a little cough. "Somewhere here."

"Somewhere here," Janet muttered. "Maybe we should do as Sada suggested and just stay in one place and wait until the mist thins. I feel like we are fish in a murky gray pond, swimming around and around in one big circle!"

Zephyr inclined her head in agreement. "In a clear night, stars will point the way home."

Janet slid off Zephyr's back. She stretched her arms high over her head, trying to rid herself of the stiffness and cold. "It will be nice to get home where it is warm and dry. I can hardly wait to be in my own bed again!"

Janet slipped the string bag from her shoulder and helped Zephyr take off the blanket roll. They went to a tall branching conifer and discovered a soft, nearly dry bed of pine needles. They spread Sada's blanket over it. Janet sat down, her back against the tree trunk. Zephyr crouched beside her, balancing on her long tail.

"What food is there, Janet nestfriend?"

Janet opened Sada's parcel and found dried mango

slices, apples, and berries tied on a string. There was also a loaf of bread studded with nuts, a sliced cassava with a paste of red pepper, and several sweet potatoes. "What would you like?" Janet asked Zephyr, who looked over the collection of food.

"Hmm," Zephyr crooned, her sharp glance taking in the assortment. The sunspots over her eyes flashed as she reached over Janet and pulled up a curled fiddle-head fern that was growing beside Janet. "This, nest-friend. Very delicious." She nibbled the fern, beginning at the root all the way to the coiled head. And as she ate, she made little pleasure sounds in her throat. "Very delicious," she repeated.

Janet laughed and chose a sweet potato and slices of nut bread. "How lucky we are, Zephyr, to have met someone like Sada," Janet said as she chewed her food. "I want to be a person like that."

"Sada has many gifts!" Zephyr replied. "And so do you, Janet. "

"I'm still scared to go home and face everybody," Janet said, picking up a piece of bread. "But I know it's the right thing to do. The Hatchery is where I belong."

As she started to bring the bread to her mouth, a deep wailing cry filled the air. Janet froze, the bread halfway to her mouth. The sound was mournful, a lone voice calling across the mist. It echoed in the fog, surrounding Janet and Zephyr.

Then it was quiet again. Janet held her breath but

heard only the soft dripping of rainwater off the leaves of the trees.

"What was that?" Janet asked in a hushed whisper.

"Not certain," answered Zephyr, straightening up. She stretched her neck high, turning her head from side to side as if to catch the fading sound in her ears.

Janet started as the cry rose again. Deeper and more hollow this time.

"Dinosaur," Zephyr announced.

"Where?" Janet asked as she stood and turned slowly in the mist. She remembered the mysterious footprint on the path and wondered if the voice belonged to its owner. In the echoing fog it was impossible to tell from which direction the cry came.

The voice cried out again, a long note that wavered in the mist. It was followed by another low note. Janet realized that the voice was singing the opening phrases of a song. The leaves vibrated as the song rumbled. Janet could catch the meaning of only two words: *lost* and *firehome*.

Zephyr's nostrils flared. She turned in a slow circle, trying to find the source of the song; then she piped a series of small, sharp throaty calls. The voice answered once more, urgency in the low cry.

"Come!" Zephyr commanded. She grabbed Janet's hand and led her swiftly through the bushes.

"What is it?" Janet asked breathlessly as she tried to keep up with Zephyr's swift steps.

"Hurt. Pain and loneliness. Song of last things.

We must help. Like Sada!"

"Last things? Zephyr, I don't understand."

The voice started again. Zephyr stopped to follow the direction of the sound. Suddenly Janet felt afraid, standing in the dense fog listening to the eerie voice that called to them. She was afraid of the unknown dinosaur hidden from her sight. What if it was injured or, worse, dying? What could she possibly do to help? She was only a girl, lost in the woods.

"Zephyr—" Janet started to say, thinking perhaps they should go back and try to find Sada. But Zephyr wasn't paying attention to her. Her eyes were a bright gold, and her blue and orange scales flashed as she tried to find the owner of the song. She ground her teeth, her back molars clicking with agitation. Zephyr sang and waited.

"There!" Zephyr squeaked as the song resumed. "That way."

Zephyr grabbed Janet's hand once more, and they plunged into the thick bushes and shrubs. Over their heads the song drifted with the fog, the voice getting louder, its direction slowly becoming more distinct. Janet understood enough words to know that it was indeed a cry for help. Someone was injured and alone in the fog. Suddenly Janet realized that even though she was afraid, she must act. Just as Sada had done for her and Zephyr the night before, she must answer the stranger's call for help in the forest.

Zephyr ducked beneath the spreading branches of

a high dark green conifer, scattering raindrops on Janet's head as she followed behind her. As Janet stopped to wipe the water out of her eyes she heard Zephyr speaking quickly, her voice a rising and falling burst of clicks and squeaks. Through the fog Janet could make out the two darker smudges of the dinosaurs. A little breeze scattered the mist for a moment, and Janet saw Zephyr speaking to a large dinosaur, the bulk of her body braced against two fallen trees.

Janet was surprised by the dinosaur, for she looked both familiar and strange at the same time. She was a hadrosaur, similar to Grass Sweeper and the Maiasaura females of the Hatchery. She had a thick, powerful neck and a large, heavy body. Her back legs were very muscular, and her smaller front arms rested over the fallen logs to keep her upright. Her coloring was oddly patched, a faded rust with deep green patches covering her sides. Her skull was shaped differently as well, with a bony ridge that circled the back of her head like a small frill of spikes. The skin appeared loose at her cheeks, and Janet saw that as the dinosaur spoke or sang, the loose skin filled with air, making a low vibrating tone that accompanied her speech.

Zephyr held her tail up stiffly in a gesture of concern as she spoke. Janet tried to follow the music of the dinosaurs' conversation, but she could understand only a few of the words. Zephyr's speech was much too quick, like the rapping of a drum, while the strange dinosaur's voice was slow, each word stretching into long syllables.

Janet didn't need the words, though, to tell her what was wrong. The female had injured her back leg. Janet could see where the bone was set at a wrong angle below the knee. Around the area the flesh had become swollen and bruised. A long gash on the dinosaur's shin was covered with dried blood. It was a serious injury to a large dinosaur, and Janet knew that there was no way they could help her alone. They would need to fetch more experienced hands from the Hatchery—and soon.

Janet approached the dinosaur's head and held out her hand in a greeting of respect. "Breathe deep, seek peace," she said.

The dinosaur looked at her kindly, but Janet could see that her eyes were clouded with pain.

The dinosaur said something to her. A long hummed word. Janet struggled to shape the sound into a meaning. The dinosaur repeated it, watching Janet carefully. Janet wondered whether the dinosaur was saying her name. Gradually, as the word was repeated, it took on a familiar ring. Suddenly, with a burst of understanding, Janet knew what the word was.

"Egg," Janet said. She turned to Zephyr. "She is with egg."

"Yes, nestfriend," Zephyr said. "She is soon to bring forth the last egg of her clan."

"The last egg?" Janet asked, confused. "Aren't there others like her?"

"No. She is the only one."

"But where does she come from?"

"Zephyr doesn't know. Her songs are old, much older than this one, and the words sometimes strange. I know only pieces. But I know what is important. It is the egg that is important."

"What shall we do?"

"Must help, Janet," Zephyr said simply. She held out her hands to Janet, the palms turned upward. "You are apprentice. You must help."

Janet stood astonished into silence by Zephyr's words. What could she, a mere apprentice, do? This was a serious problem even for a master. What did Zephyr want her to do? The injured dinosaur stared at Janet from weary eyes.

All Janet could think of was that she had been a dismal failure in her job before. But who else was there?

"Come, Janet, give me your hands," Zephyr encouraged. "She needs your help."

CHAPTER 6

"Oh, Zephyr, I can't do this," Janet protested when she found her voice again. "I don't know nearly enough yet. We must go back to the farm and get real help."

"Stay and use what you know," Zephyr said. "I will return to the Hatchery. When stars are out, I will travel. Then return with others here. You, nestfriend, stay and help. There is no other way. Have courage."

Janet's hands trembled as she laid her palms on Zephyr's hands. "Aye," she agreed solemnly. "I'll do what I can."

"It is good."

Janet drew in a shaky breath and turned back to face the injured dinosaur. "Called am I, Janet," she said. "Though new from the egg, I will try to help you. Please, good mother, give me the knowledge of your name that I may speak with respect."

The hadrosaur listened, her head tilted to one side as if to catch the strange-sounding words Janet offered. At last she nodded slowly at Janet and drew in a deep, slow breath. As she exhaled, she sang a name. "Kranog, shining sun am I." And then she sang another phrase, her cheek pouches making a low humming sound. Janet understood only one word of the phrase, and that was the word *hope*.

"I may examine you, Kranog?" Janet asked.

Again the hadrosaur listened and nodded. Janet ran her hands lightly over the neck and the shoulders of the dinosaur. Her thick scaled skin was dry to the touch and had deep scratches in it, as if she had been traveling a long time through the difficult forest.

Janet tried to remember everything that Fatherfast had taught her. Surely there was something in her learning that she could use here. She continued moving her hands gently over Kranog, feeling the hadrosaur's muscles tense against the pain. Janet could ease some of the discomfort with massage and heated moss and mud packs. The gash she could clean, and there were herbs in the forest that she could use to dress the wound to keep it free of infection. But the injured leg was far more serious than anything Janet knew how to mend.

Janet felt along Kranog's sides. The slack skin meant that the dinosaur needed food and water. She hadn't been able to forage on her injured leg. Janet would have to find food for her so that she could keep up her strength while they waited for Zephyr to return.

"Kranog, the shining sun, I think I can help ease this pain," Janet said.

"Moon to stars," Kranog replied in her low rumbling voice.

"What does she mean?" Janet asked Zephyr.

"An old compliment. Your goodness shines very bright, like the moon that outshines the small stars."

"Thank you," Janet said to Kranog, blushing. Then she turned to Zephyr, her face serious. "Kranog needs food. I don't know when she last ate." Janet began counting off items on her fingers. "We need water, club mosses, and *Arctium longevus* for her wound."

"Food I will get," Zephyr offered.

From the low-lying bushes Zephyr gathered sweet green ferns and branches, which she brought to Kranog. Kranog gladly took them, chewing slowly as though savoring every bite of the green plants. Janet searched for *Arctium longevus,* a common plant found on Dinotopia that had many uses. She knew that when brewed into tea, the plant helped to prolong life, especially for humans. But it also served to promote fast healing in cuts and deep wounds. When crushed, the purple flowers brought heat to the surrounding area, which helped to numb the pain of a gash.

Janet collected the tall flowering plant where it grew in little stands. She used Sada's string bag to gather clumps of wet mosses, planning to wring the water out of them later. She made sure that she kept within earshot of Kranog's deep singing. She knew that as long as she could hear the dinosaur's voice, she could find her way back to camp.

While she hunted for her supplies, Janet's mind raced ahead, trying to list all the things she would need. By nightfall she would have to make a fire. She had a small silver box from the Hatchery with a flint, steel, and tinder made of bark shavings. Janet chewed her lip and worried. She had learned, as every apprentice must, how to start a fire. But it didn't always work for her. And she wondered where in this wet, misty forest she would find wood dry enough to burn. And then there was the problem of a container. She needed to heat water to clean Kranog's wounds and then to create a mash of *Arctium longevus* to put over the wound and seal it.

Janet was thinking so hard that she didn't look where she was walking and tripped over a scattered pile of loose rocks. At first she was angry, her knees aching and bruised where she had fallen. But the rocks gave her an idea. She gathered as many as she could and brought them back to Kranog. Janet smiled when she saw that the food was already helping Kranog's condition. The dinosaur's rust-colored scales were brightening to a healthy crimson.

"Can you help me with this?" Janet asked Zephyr as she stacked the rocks in a circle. "I need as many as I can get to build a fire in this wet place. Also, if you find any rocks hollowed enough to hold water, maybe I can use them."

"You are right, Janet. I have seen some that will work well. I will bring them."

"Good," Janet said. She wiped her damp hair from her face, leaving a smear of mud on her forehead. "I'll get started here."

Janet tore up plants until she had exposed a circle of earth. Then she set the stones in the circle. She headed back into the surrounding forest to search for more. When she returned, Zephyr appeared from between the trees. Her arms were full of stones. Together they built a small wall of stones. Then Janet retrieved the driest of the pine needles, twigs, and pine cones from beneath the conifers. These she brought back to the circle of stones and set them in the middle.

Using her flint and tinder, she took a deep breath and began to start a fire. *Remember,* she could hear her father saying, *be patient. Strike the sparks toward the heart of the tinder, and it will start.*

Janet struck the steel with the flint, and little sparks leaped toward the bark shavings. Janet leaned forward, hoping that one of the sparks had caught in the shavings. But there was nothing. Not even a hint of smoke. She tried again, striking the flint just as her father had shown her. Again the sparks leaped from the flint to the tinder. This time one tiny spark caught in the bark like a jewel and began to smoke.

Don't rush now, Janet heard her father say. *The spark is small. Blow gently.*

Janet resisted the urge to blow all of her hope and fear into the little spark. Instead she puffed lightly, encouraging the spark to blossom into fire. It flared brighter, and another bark shaving caught fire. Smoke curled up in a thin, pale thread. Still blowing gently, Janet fed the growing fire some pine needles. These burned quickly and made lively snapping sounds. She gave the hungry fire more pine needles and then twigs. When she had a small bed of coals, she added the pine cones, which cracked loudly in the moist air. Seeds popped from beneath the scales and scattered over the stones as the pine cones burned.

"Look, Janet, I have found wood," Zephyr called. Janet looked up and saw Zephyr struggling under the weight of an armload of nearly dry logs. She jumped up and went to help.

"Oh, Zephyr, this is wonderful. Just what I needed!" Janet exclaimed as she carefully laid two small logs over the fire.

The damp bark hissed and steamed. Then the underside of one of the logs caught fire, and bright yellow flames licked up the sides of the logs. Janet sat back on her heels and held her cold hands out to the fire.

"Where did you find the wood?" she asked Zephyr.

"Same place I found this," Zephyr said, showing Janet a clay bowl. It was an earthy color with a pattern of black leaves. There was a chip on the rim, but it was solid enough to hold water. "From an old house that is no more than bones. The dry wood and bowl had been left behind."

"It's perfect, Zephyr," Janet said happily.

She took the soggy moss and began to squeeze the clumps over the bowl. There was enough water in the moss to almost fill the bowl. She made a platform of rocks over some of the hot coals and set about heating the water. She added the purple flowers and *Arctium longevus* leaves to the water and stirred it with a stick. When the water was steaming she tore a part of the hem from her tunic and dipped it into the hot water. Then she placed the bowl of water beside Kranog's injured leg.

"Kranog, I need to wash your wound. It will hurt, but it must be done," Janet said.

Kranog lowered her head toward Janet and sighed deeply. "It must be done," she repeated slowly, as if practicing the strange words.

Janet washed the wound clean of dirt and dried blood. She tried to be thorough, as Fatherfast had taught her. The torn gash was deep and needed to be closed with silk stitches, but Janet didn't have the supplies. So instead of stitches, she tore another piece off the hem of her tunic. Then she applied the warm mash of flowers and *Arctium longevus* leaves to Kranog's leg and wrapped the cloth over it.

"There," Janet said as she finished. "Does it feel better, Kranog?" she asked hopefully.

Kranog turned to gaze at Janet. Her eyes were clearer now, a jade green color, and they sparkled with intelligence. "Better?" she rumbled.

Zephyr scratched her neck and quickly spoke a few words.

"Ah…" Kranog sighed with understanding. She inclined her head again toward Janet. "Green is the branch after the time of long drying. Sand finds sun, there is heat. Water sings in streams."

Janet listened transfixed by the strange beauty of Kranog's reply. Her low voice trembled, and the solemn sound of it filled the misty forest like a warm invitation.

"I understand some of the words, but not always the meaning," Janet said to Zephyr.

"You asked if she was better, nestfriend," Zephyr said, feeding a small log into the fire.

"Aye, I did."

"And she sang to you of those things that are welcomed after the cold drought of her home. The leaves that return, the water in the streams, the sand that heats up in the summer sun. She feels one with those things. It is how she says she is 'better.' Do you understand now?" Zephyr asked.

"I'm beginning to," Janet answered.

Janet and Zephyr continued to gather branches and ferns for Kranog to eat. Janet went to the vine-covered remains of the old cottage and searched for other things that might be useful. Besides a store of firewood and a wooden spoon, she didn't find anything else. It made her sad to see the cottage of rotted wood and moss-covered rocks in the damp forest. She wondered who had lived there and why they had left. Perhaps, unlike Sada, they had found the woods too quiet and lonely.

When evening came, they were still surrounded by fog. But the glow of the fire cheered them and kept them warm and dry despite the chilly night. Janet heated more water and soaked moss in it. Then she carried the moss to Kranog and squeezed the warm water over Kranog's shoulders, cleaning the other scrapes and cuts on her skin. Kranog's voice rumbled appreciatively at the splash of warm water over her shoulders and spine.

"Song fills the mouth, swallowed to the heart. Then still as the sun's rising over the mountain," Kranog murmured.

Zephyr started to speak, but Janet stopped her with a hand.

"I understand it," she said. "'Song fills the mouth'—it means 'breathe deep.' And 'still as the sun's rising'—it's the same as 'seek peace.' It's Kranog's way of saying 'breathe deep, seek peace.'"

"You are right, Janet," Zephyr said and her scales flashed with happiness. "But now it also means we must rest. Sleep, Janet. I will watch for stars to come."

Janet rolled herself in Sada's brightly colored blanket and lay beside the fire. She listened to Kranog's quiet breathing, the dinosaur's cheek pouches humming softly as she exhaled. It made the night forest seem restful and safe. Closing her eyes, Janet slept.

It seemed only moments later when Zephyr shook her on the shoulder. Janet opened her eyes to see the scattered stars twinkling in the black night sky.

"I must go now," Zephyr said. "The stars will show me the way home."

"Which stars?" Janet asked, sleepily gazing up at the dazzling sight.

"See those two nestfriend stars? Above the tree?" Zephyr pointed to a pair of bright blue-green stars.

"Aye, I see them," Janet answered, rubbing the sleep from her eyes.

"The Hatchery is there. Just beneath those two stars. I will follow them and return with help soon. Will it be well with you, Janet?" Zephyr asked, taking Janet's hands between her palms.

"Aye," Janet replied, sounding braver than she felt. "We'll be fine. But hurry, Zephyr."

"Like wind I go."

Zephyr released Janet's hands and headed into the woods. Janet watched her leave, a swift shadow that disappeared suddenly into the dark forest. Kranog napped by the fire, still humming her slow resting song. Janet lay down again and stared up at the nestfriend stars.

CHAPTER 7

The sky had faded from midnight blue to dawn gray when Janet awoke again to a loud rustling noise. Janet sat up quickly. Kranog was trying to walk away from her perch of fallen logs.

"No, Kranog," Janet called to stop her. "You will make it worse. Zephyr will be back with help soon."

"Hearth home, sand calls, circle of life," Kranog answered, her cheek pouches making loud sharp blasts like a trumpet.

"I don't understand!" Janet said, frustrated by the strangeness of Kranog's words. The wound on Kranog's leg was beginning to bleed again, the blood staining the bandage as she tried to walk. "Kranog, shining sun, I ask that you be calm," Janet tried again.

"Janet, hearth home. Egg to the center. Away!" In the pale morning light Kranog's skin flashed crimson. She raised her head to the stars as if catching the scent of a faraway place. She was breathing hard, and her tail slapped the low bushes.

"Wait!" Janet cried. "I know what it is. The egg—"

Kranog stopped struggling and leaned heavily

71

against a tree. She looked at Janet determinedly.

"You want to lay your last egg at home," Janet said.

Kranog sighed deeply, the long humming of her cheek pouches sounding as sad as it had the day before in the mist. "Hearth home, circled sand. Earth and egg centered."

"Can you wait until Zephyr has returned?"

"No. Egg gathers. Sand calls. My home." Kranog began to move again.

"Stop, Kranog," Janet called, her hands held out in a gesture of respect. "You're injured. The egg will suffer. You will suffer. Wait. Just one more day."

Kranog looked into the sky where the last star faded with the promise of the coming sunrise. "Time is passed. Stars to new sun. Janet help Kranog. Help home. Of my clan, egg must be in circle of sand."

Janet nodded, the meaning of Kranog's words sinking in at last. "I understand now, Kranog. This is the last egg of your clan. If it is laid at home, in the circle of sand, it will always know home, no matter where it goes later. It will know in its heart the place to which its whole family once belonged. And to know where one belongs," she said, thinking of the Hatchery, "is important. I'll help you. But tell me, Kranog, is home far?"

"Beyond the back teeth in earth's mouth," she replied. "Curl of earth's gold tongue. Flaming nostrils breathing into the sky."

"Great," Janet muttered to herself. "A riddle for an answer."

Janet glanced at the remains of their camp. She had to leave a message for Zephyr. The black shards of charcoal in the old fire gave Janet an idea. She cleared another patch of earth and, charcoal in hand, began to write Kranog's words in Dinotopian script.

"Now, you must not put weight on your leg or you will hurt yourself even more," Janet told Kranog.

"Tree," Kranog said, and pointed her chin toward the fallen tree logs.

"Of course!" Janet answered.

Janet pulled on her boots and went to the fallen logs. She placed then on the ground, near Kranog, the shorter, thinner one near the top of the longer one. She tore fabric from the hem of her cape and wound the woolen fabric around the two logs to make a crutch. It was crude and bulky. But Kranog was able to tuck it under her front forearm and walk with it.

"I hope the crutch makes it all the way," Janet said worriedly.

"Away. Away," Kranog called, giving a high bugle.

"I'm coming," Janet answered.

Janet quickly gathered up her things, tied her cape onto her shoulders, and then rolled up the blanket. Janet was grateful to Sada for giving them the extra supplies. Janet couldn't imagine what she would have done without them. She had learned many lessons in the last few days, she thought. The first was to face mistakes with a brave heart. The second was not to rush into a fog. The third was to always pack extra for the journey. And the last was never to underestimate the speed of an injured but determined dinosaur.

Janet hurried after Kranog, following the bugling song Kranog sang as she marched through the green forest. They traveled all morning through fan-leafed ginkgoes and conifers. Amid the deep green of the forest were huge shrubs covered with big pink and lavender blooms that amazed Janet with their brilliance. Orchids clung to the shaggy bark of cycads, catching water droplets in their creamy blossoms. The sun rising above the tall trees sent arrows of gold light between the crowded branches.

Kranog never wavered from her direction. Janet knew that instinct was guiding Kranog through the forest. The map was inside her, as clear as the stars that were leading Zephyr back to the Hatchery.

As midday approached, Kranog stopped and turned to Janet. She was breathing hard from the fast pace she had set despite her injury. Janet could see that her skin had faded to its tired rust color again. But her eyes were still a clear jade green.

"Speak," Kranog said to Janet.

"About what?" Janet asked, breathless herself from trying to keep up. The land was sloping beneath her feet and, though the forest was still dense, Janet sensed that they were climbing a mountain.

"All things. Songs, words. Kranog listen. Wings to the journey."

"All right," Janet agreed.

As they continued, Janet sang the songs that she had learned as a very young child. These were mostly silly songs about how to tie your shoes, or do sums, or know the different hours in the day. When she couldn't think of any more, Janet began to sing the songs that Zephyr had taught her when they played together. Some of these songs told the deeds of famous dinosaurs and humans in the history of Dinotopia; others sang about the beauty of the land. Janet remembered a few love songs and then one long poem about the Ring Riding races in Cornucopia. And still they climbed through the forest.

"More," Kranog said.

Tired of singing, Janet switched to telling the old stories that her mother had told her, stories of creatures with pale green faces and the gift of magic. Then she told her father's stories of the galleons that once sailed the oceans in search of new worlds. She told classic tales about the simple fool who turned into a wise man, and the Hatchery girl who tried to capture the moon by lifting its reflection out of a stream with a spoon. All day long Janet kept up a constant flow and chatter of words. Kranog said nothing, only listened, occasionally making a soft low noise to show that she was pleased or surprised by something Janet said.

The day faded, the long shadows falling over the forest again. When the edge of the new moon peeked over the top of the trees, Kranog suddenly stopped walking. She leaned her body against a natural ledge of rock.

"Janet, journey friend, here we rest. Your body must now feel tired. Make a good fire. Get warm. We have traveled far on this day's journey."

Janet stared in weary confusion at Kranog. "Kranog, I've been talking all day. But it seems as if I can understand you better, even though you've said nothing since morning. How can that be?"

Kranog gave a short blasting sound, and Janet realized that Kranog was laughing. "Aye, Janet. I can now speak as you do. Once was I a teacher of languages. I spoke and read many languages, some almost like yours. But it has been many seasons since this one has heard these sounds. Easy they are to forget. But on this day's journey I listened and learned again. Heard the pattern like song that your words make. Hope will I to make it easier for us."

Janet sat down, astonished. "You're a teacher?"

"Long ago, when there were schools and lessons to be taught. Now much is gone. Make a fire, Janet. We must have warmth. This night will be colder than the other. We have come higher up the mountains," Kranog said.

Janet set about making a fire. The wood was dry here, and the sparks flew from the flint to the tinder.

Soon flames were flickering up to the velvety night sky. She made a tea from the *Arctium longevus* and gave some to Kranog to drink out of the bowl. Then she gathered more leaves and branches for the dinosaur. Janet checked the wound and was worried by the sight of new blood.

"I must clean your wound again, Kranog."

"It is well enough, Janet. You must eat and keep your strength whole. The journey is only a little ways done. And the homecoming for you will be harder."

"What do you mean?" Janet asked, confused.

Kranog gave a low-throated sigh. "There is no one to welcome us at my home, Janet. It will be difficult."

"Where have they gone?"

"Away. Many years ago these valleys were filled with my clan, the Saurolophus. But our world changed, and we could no longer live there. This you will see. But first, Janet, tell me of you. Tell me of your home and your family."

Janet opened her food pack and took out Sada's bread. It was a little stale and dried out, but it tasted delicious to Janet's hungry stomach. She set the bowl on the fire and made some tea. In between bites of food and sips of tea, Janet told Kranog stories about her mother and father—how they had met at a haying party, courted, and then married. She told Kranog about her grandparents, who were both Hatchery farmers, and her great-grandfather, who had traveled all over Dinotopia as a weaver. She told stories about her many cousins and aunts and uncles.

"And have you other nestlings?" Kranog asked.

"No. I've no brothers or sisters."

"Like this egg. But still you have a family of which you are proud."

"Aye, that is true," Janet said. She was proud of her family, and surprised that she could remember so many stories of their lives. It was a pleasant tradition for every child on the farm to share with her nest-friend the history of her family.

"And does Zephyr tell you her family tales as well?" Kranog asked.

"Oh, aye." Janet laughed. "But there I get very confused. The names are so long sometimes I get them twisted around my tongue. But I have managed to learn quite a few of them."

"Speak to me of them," Kranog said.

Janet took a big breath and tried to recall the ones she had learned. Zephyr had stressed the importance to her of learning the dinosaur names well. Better to remember three absolutely right than twenty that were almost right, she once told Janet. Janet knew that lineage was important to the dinosaurs, and they treasured the old names like family jewels. She sang the ten that she knew she remembered well. "Fire-over-grass, Song-of-red-throat-in-green." These were the dinosaur names of Zephyr's immediate family. "Far-into-golcha-n-tern" and "Bri-chur-crik-ah" were two of the names in the old language that Janet didn't understand.

Kranog listened, her head nodding to the sound of the names, acknowledging each one. She hummed a slow drone of respect in her throat as Janet listed the names.

"And you, Kranog?" Janet asked when she was at last finished. "Tell me the names of your lineage."

Kranog inhaled deeply. She raised her face to the sky and began to sing very slowly. Her voice was solemn and vibrated like the low notes of a cello. Even the stars hovering in the night sky seemed to tremble with the song. Janet hugged herself around her knees and wanted to cry at the slow singing of the names. They were all gone, she realized with sadness. And only Kranog was left to remember them…Kranog and the egg that was coming.

When Kranog finished singing, she lowered her head and was silent for a moment. Around them the wind whispered through the leaves of the tree branches. Then Kranog looked up again at Janet. Firelight sparkled in her eyes.

"Janet, journey friend, would you do me a great honor?"

"Aye, of course," Janet answered, surprised to be asked such a question.

"Let me teach you the singing of our names so that their stories will not be lost. So that other voices besides mine may bring them into the future."

"Kranog, the shining one, it is I who will be honored to learn such names," Janet said softly. "I am your student."

"It is nice to have one again," Kranog said. "Begin will I with the first mothers."

Kranog sang a name, and then waited for Janet to repeat it. Then she sang another name, and Janet sang the first name and then the second. They sang back and forth, Janet trying hard to learn the many names and their correct order. Sometimes it seemed easy, the sounds of the names rolling smoothly off her tongue like washed pebbles. Other times, when the names sounded like a cough, it was hard to get the sound exactly right. Finally, well into the night, Janet was too weary to remember what she was singing. Her eyelids began to close, and her chin drooped to her chest.

"It is enough, Janet," Kranog said gently. "Sleep now, and sing will I into your dreams."

Janet curled up in her blanket and closed her eyes. But she continued to hear the sounds of Kranog's low voice singing the names of her lineage.

On the following day they reached the crest of the mountain. As they traveled along its spine, Janet saw that it was one of many mountains forming a long ridge. Here there were tall cliffs of weathered rocks and stunted trees whose trunks were twisted and bent away from the wind. Along the path the grass formed fat pillows of gray-green. Small streams trickled over the rocks, and squat pine trees were topped with shaggy heads of rough leaves. The air was dry and cold, and her breath came in little white puffs as she trudged beside Kranog. And though the climb had been difficult, Janet paid little attention as she worked to remember the names of Kranog's lineage. She practiced singing the names and every now and then Kranog would stop to correct her gently.

As she marched Janet was concentrating so hard on the song of names, staring at the tips of her boots, that she scarcely noticed when they left the spine of the mountain and began to travel down the other side.

"Look, Janet. See below how it shines," Kranog said, stopping to lean heavily on her crutch. With one hand she gestured to the valley below the mountain.

Janet looked up and gasped at the sight. Down the green mountainside the forests suddenly ended, and below them stretched a wide valley of yellow grass. The wind blew over it, and the swaying grass looked like the waves of a golden sea. The sun that was blocked by the shadow of trees on the mountainside was bright on the land below. The sky was a clear blue. On the other side of the wide plain Janet could just make out the rise of a single broad mountain capped with snow. The lower slopes of the mountain were streaked a dark coal color. At the base of the mountain there were two strange smaller peaks nearly hidden in a cloud of gray smoke.

"How beautiful," Janet whispered at the sight of the golden plains. "But what is that on the other side of the plains? At the bottom of the mountain? It looks like a Hatchery chimney!"

"Home," Kranog said, and Janet heard the note of sadness in Kranog's voice. "Come, hurry. The circle waits, but the egg does not. Weary am I growing of the journey."

They continued to make their way down the side of the mountain, the sparse trees growing thick again as they reached the lower side of the mountain. Flowers bloomed around them, from pale pink to a deep blue. One shrub was covered with clusters of little white flowers and tiny blue-black berries. Kranog stopped and gestured to the bush.

"Here, Janet, pick from these. They are sweet and will give you strength. Gather as many as you can."

Janet picked the berries, popping a few in her mouth as she did. The skin was tart at first, but the flesh underneath was indeed very sweet. Janet realized how hungry and tired she was from the day's climb. For every berry she gathered, she ate two, letting the sweet juice fill her mouth and run down her throat.

"Here, too," Kranog called, and pointed out another plant growing low to the ground. It was a single orange and yellow flower raised out of a bunch of thick flat leaves. "Dig, and its root will please you. But remember to leave some behind that the plant will continue to grow."

Janet dug the soft soil and pulled up a few of the roots. They were like fat little radishes covered with dirt. She brushed them clean and ate one. It tasted a bit like one of Sada's sweet potatoes. "These are good!" Janet exclaimed.

"There is much to eat in the forest. But do not eat any white berries. They will make you ill. And now I think this is a good place to camp for us."

"But we are so close to your home," Janet said, confused.

"The valley is wider than it looks. It will take most of a morning to cross it. And this day is fast to leave us already. Once on the plains there is no water to find and nowhere for this one to rest. So tomorrow we will go."

Janet set up camp again, pleased at how quickly she could now use her flint to make a fire. She gathered water from a small trickling stream and set it to boil.

"You must let me tend to your wound," Janet insisted.

Kranog shook her head. "It is enough. I feel no pain there anymore."

"Are you sure?" Janet asked.

"Sing to me the names of my family. Let me feel better knowing that you are remembering," Kranog said.

Janet hesitated, wanting to argue with Kranog. But she sensed that hearing the names was far more important to Kranog now than her wound. Almost as important as the egg that she carried. So Janet began to sing the names. She sang all the way through four generations of names before she made her first mistake.

"Oh, dear," she said, feeling discouraged. "I thought I knew them better."

"But you are a good student indeed," Kranog said. "I am well pleased by your skill."

"Thank you. But I hope I can get them all correct."

"Practice. And they will always be with you," Kranog said gently. Then she blew soft notes through her cheek pouches. "Sleep, Janet. The day will be long again."

Janet pulled the folds of her blanket around her shoulders and stared at the stars. To her sleepy eyes it looked as if the sky were filled with the starry outlines of hundreds of dinosaurs. In her mind she gave them the names of Kranog's ancestors.

CHAPTER 8

Kranog woke Janet with a soft bugling. The sun had not yet broken over the horizon, and Janet did not want to get up. Her limbs were tired from the long march the day before. She peeked out at the gray dawn light and groaned.

"We must go now, before the sun is too hot on the plains," Kranog explained.

"All right," Janet agreed, yawning.

She quickly packed and then fell into line behind Kranog. Janet was worried about the dinosaur. Her color was again a pale rust, and her skin hung in loose folds. She leaned heavily on the crutch, which showed new cracks. What would happen if the crutch broke on the plains? Janet wondered. But Kranog continued to move quickly, and sometimes Janet had to trot to keep up.

All at once, they stepped from the shelter of the mountain's trees and entered the plains. Janet squinted against the sudden brilliance of the morning sunlight on the golden grass. She stared in surprise, for what she had thought was a golden field of grass was no more than old straw, preserved in the dry mountain air. It wasn't a living plain, but a desert. The wind made a rustling sound through the dry grass as it chased across the valley.

As they walked onto the plains, Janet and Kranog cut a narrow path through the rustling grass. Overhead the sky was a huge blue bowl. There were no clouds, but over Kranog's mountain home the moon hung like a pale ghost in the blue sky. Janet turned to look back at the mountain ridge they had crossed. The gray flat-topped rocks of the peaks looked like old teeth rising out of the gums of the earth. She turned around in the golden grass to look at the twin smoking peaks. Suddenly she laughed.

"What is giving you humor?" Kranog asked.

"I have the answer to a riddle. You said you lived where the back teeth of the earth met the gold tongue. Those mountains there, they look like teeth. And this plain, it's like a golden tongue. And there, the two little mountains with smoke, those are the nostrils, aren't they?"

"Aye, you are right, Janet." Kranog looked out at the twin peaks. "There will we find home."

By the time Janet and Kranog reached the other side of the plains, the sun was high in the sky, and the wind hot and dry as an open oven. Janet could see the faint outline of a path between the two small smoking mountains as they neared them. Janet was tired and footsore. Her lips and throat were parched from the dry wind of the plains. And now, close to Kranog's home, she was not comforted by what she saw.

The twin peaks were new volcanoes, and their smoking cones were ringed with black ash and dried lava. Slowly they walked up the hillside to the path that led between the peaks. Janet felt the land tremble and rumble beneath her feet. The air was dense with grit and smelled of sulfur.

"Come, Janet. This was once my home and the home of our people. Rivers once ran through this valley, but no more," Kranog said as she led the way between the two smoking peaks.

The sun continued to beat down on them as they traveled between the two peaks. Janet realized that they were walking up the path of an old streambed. Bushes and grasses had dried and curled into bundled sticks and straw. They passed a stand of skeleton trees and a plow abandoned in the black soil.

The ground continued to tremble and shake with small tremors. Steam hissed at them from cracks. When they reached the other side of the smoking peaks, Janet saw the remains of Kranog's city.

Wide stairs had been carved into the wall of the mountain. They led up into the cliffs, where empty windows peered down from large houses nestled into the mountain. Judging from the size of the doors, Janet knew that humans had lived there once. She marveled at the sculptures of birds and dinosaurs that lined the stairway up into the city. In the slanting rays of the afternoon sun she could see the faded paintings on the walls of the houses.

Kranog stopped for a moment to stare up at the lonely city. "Come, into the residence," she said.

Kranog led the way to a row of wide-mouthed caves that lay along the base of the mountain. These were rooms that had been carved into the mountain, large enough for the biggest dinosaurs to go into. Janet looked with fascination over the arched doorways. Dinosaur script had been carved into the stone walls. She could read some of the words and realized that these spacious residences served as Hatcheries for Kranog's ancestors.

Kranog, with a sudden spurt of strength, went eagerly into a room higher up on the mountain. But she moved awkwardly, her body weary from the long journey. Her tail dragged heavily behind her, digging a trench in the sand. As she crossed the threshold into the residence, her crutch snapped and splintered beneath her sagging weight. Without her crutch, Kranog fell on her injured leg with a blasting cry of pain.

Janet ran to catch up to her. But by the time she had reached Kranog, the dinosaur had straightened herself as best she could. Janet was alarmed by the ashy color of the dinosaur and her shallow breathing.

"Do not fear for me, Janet. I am home," Kranog said, her voice croaking dryly. "See where I will lay this last egg."

Kranog limped over to a hollowed circle of sand. A carved stone bench lay across it to hold the mother dinosaur as she awaited the coming of her egg. A perch was built into the wall like a shelf on which the dinosaur could rest her head. Spiral patterns had been painted over the floor of the hollowed nesting circle. Kranog laid her body on the hatching bench and then wearily rested her chin on the perch.

As Janet watched, Kranog seemed to grow thin before her eyes. Her scales became as dull as sand. The effort of coming home had taken all of Kranog's strength. All she had left to do was await the coming of her egg. Janet tried to beat back her worry, wishing she knew more and could help Kranog.

"To the back of the residence there are springs. Once they ran clean and pure through the whole mountain and these caves. The steam and moist heat aided in the incubation of our eggs. The volcanoes dried up most of the springs. But perhaps there is a little water remaining for you, Janet. You must have a great thirst after the dryness of the plains."

"I will look," Janet said, "and bring us some back."

"Aye," Kranog said, and then began to hum softly.

The low murmuring sound echoed in the cave and made Janet feel at peace. She walked to the back of Kranog's cave, staring at the paintings on the high curved walls. There were scenes of everyday life—farmers and dinosaurs in fields of green grass, people wading into the rivers to plant green rushes, dinosaurs and people building the cliff dwellings and teaching in great houses of learning. Janet wandered from cave to cave, learning about the cave community from its paintings, marveling at the skill of the craftsmen who had built these Hatcheries.

In a third cave she found a stone basin, and a small trickle of water bubbled up from below the earth. She scooped up the water in her hands and drank it eagerly. It was cold and refreshing. She filled the bowl with water and returned to Kranog, who was resting on her perch, still humming softly to herself.

"Ah, it is good," Kranog sighed as she sipped the water. "And now, Janet, I must ask you to lay a bed of damp moss for my egg."

Janet took the moss from her string bag and soaked it in the water. A stone bowl lay beneath the dinosaur's perch to hold the newly laid egg. Janet spread the damp moss over the bottom of the bowl to make a soft nest for the new egg.

"I'll get more water," Janet said. "In this dry heat we will need more moisture to keep the egg from getting too hot."

"Aye," said Kranog faintly.

At the spring, Janet felt the first hard tremor of the earth. She clutched at the basin as the land bucked and moved beneath her feet. Stones fell from cracks in the ceiling of the cave. Quickly she ran back to Kranog, her arms over her head as dirt showered down on her. The land groaned and then fell silent.

"Kranog, are you all right?" Janet called frantically

as she entered the cave. Dust swirled in the air, making it hard to see.

"Aye. Well enough," came Kranog's answer. "Look, Janet," she said, lifting her head with effort and turning to look behind her. "Here is my egg. Born to the sand of my home."

Janet went to the egg which lay perfectly centered like an oval moon in the bed of moss. She stroked the dinosaur lovingly. "How happy am I for you, Kranog."

"And happy am I that I found you, Janet, journey friend. But there is more that I would ask of you."

The land rumbled again, and they braced as small stones tumbled down from the ceiling.

"This place is no longer safe. It is what drove our community to leave here. Only a few of us remained, hoping the land would grow stable again," Kranog explained. "Even I knew this place had changed beyond our hopes. I was trying to join with others when I fell in the forest." Her voice was faint, and Janet had to bend her head to hear the raspy words. "My love for here was too strong. Home I came. But now is it over. You must take my egg and return to the Hatchery of your family, Janet."

"No!" Janet cried. "I won't leave you."

"You must! Or we will all die, and my journey will have been for nothing."

"I can't." Janet felt the tears start in her eyes. "I can't, Kranog. I am not strong enough. Not wise enough to do this."

"There is no one else, Janet. In you do I trust. You have courage. You must use it, for me and for this egg. Zephyr will come for me. Others will help me in a day or so. But only you can help my egg. Take it from this place of danger that I may know it is safe. Take it to a new home. Take it to your Hatchery."

"No," Janet said, and covered her face with her hands. Tears burned in her eyes. "I won't leave you alone."

"I will think of you and my egg. And I will not feel lonely. Listen, Janet," Kranog continued. "Among dinosaurs there is a vow of friendship that once taken cannot be broken. It is called Gar-en-doc, or the 'shared eye.' It means that we share a vision. For me it is the vision of the future and my egg. Share it with me. Take this vow, and then take my egg to your home."

Janet wanted to refuse. She wanted to explain how scared she was. She didn't feel worthy of being entrusted with this last egg of Kranog's family.

Janet pulled her hands from her face and looked at Kranog. Her body was weakened by her journey, but her eyes glowed a bright jade green. Janet was humbled by Kranog's strength and love. She must reach for the strength that was in herself.

"I swear," said Janet softly.

"It is good." Kranog sighed. "Bring me water and *Arctium longevus*. I will wait here until the others arrive. But you must go now."

Janet reached out to touch Kranog, tears flowing over her cheeks. She wanted to protest. But the earth shifted again, the ground heaving beneath Janet's feet. The egg rolled from side to side in the moss.

"Quickly, Janet," Kranog urged.

Janet removed all the branches of *Arctium longevus* and laid it on the head perch where Kranog could reach it. She went to the spring and refilled the bowl as the dust crumbled from the trembling ceiling.

"Are you sure there is no other way?" Janet asked when she returned to Kranog.

"No other way. Go now. Travel the plains in the night. We will see each other again and celebrate your journey."

Janet carefully wrapped the egg in damp moss and put it into the string bag. She slung it over her shoulder and closed her cape to keep the egg warm on her chest. A fissure opened in the floor of the cave, and gritty smoke filled the room.

"Go. I may endure this, but you cannot," Kranog said.

"I'll see you again, Kranog, the shining sun," Janet said, hesitating at the entrance to the cave.

"And I you, Janet, journey friend," Kranog replied.

With one arm around the egg and the other shielding her tearing eyes, Janet ran.

CHAPTER 9

Janet ran over the path between the volcanoes, down the slope toward the plains. Sometimes she had to slow to a trot, then speed up again when she heard the rumbling of the twin peaks behind her. A thick cloud of smoke seemed to chase her along the dried streambed. When she couldn't run anymore she dropped to her knees in the black earth, panting. Her cheeks were hot, and the blood pounded in her ears. She pressed her hand against a painful stitch in her side as she looked around. She had almost reached the edge of the wide plain.

Janet sat on the ground and looked out over the plain of dried grass which fanned out across the wide valley like flames in the setting sun. The mountains beyond seemed far away. Janet wondered if she could cross the valley alone.

Janet checked on Kranog's egg, which was snug in its bed of damp moss in the string bag. Janet pulled out a handful of berries from beneath the egg. After she ate them, a few dried berries and mangoes would be all that remained. Would it be enough to give her the strength to cross the plain?

It would have to be, Janet decided, and carefully ate two of the fresh berries. They were sweet and juicy, and she savored them like a feast. She put the string bag with its precious cargo inside her shirt to keep the egg warm and then wrapped her shawl around her. Lying on her back, she stared up at the first of the evening stars. At the sight of the two nest-friend stars, she started to cry. She missed home, she missed Zephyr, and she missed Kranog. She cradled the egg and sang a little song to cheer herself. Then she closed her eyes and finally slept awhile.

Janet woke to a beautiful starry sky. The wind was cool, with the faintest hint of moisture carried down from the snowy heights of the mountain. Janet sat up, her body stiff and aching from the long run. She peeked at the egg, relieved to feel that it was still damp and very warm inside her shirt. Janet stood, remembering Kranog's last advice: It would be better to cross the grassy desert during the night when the air was cooler. Janet knew she would soon need water. And food. And that was possible only when she reached the far mountains again.

Janet adjusted the string bag around her neck and set off across the plain. Her legs were weary at first, her toes blistering inside her boots. To take her mind off the long journey, Janet practiced singing the names of Kranog's family lineage. As she walked she grew less tired, the rhythm of her singing carrying her through the dry desert grass. She glanced up at the stars, and they twinkled brightly, giving her courage. The new moon lay like a finger pointing the way home.

All through her night journey Janet sang. And each time she repeated the list of names, they sank deeper into her memory. At last she felt as if she knew them within her heart, their names giving descriptions of their personalities and their deeds. She realized that not only did she carry Kranog's egg, but the history of her family as well. This egg and the song of names were the last treasures to leave the old city.

In the lavender light of dawn, Janet's feet kicked a stone and then found a patch of green grass. She stopped singing. She had finally reached the end of the desert. She walked up the gentle slope into the mountains, hearing the lovely trickle of water. Her voice was hoarse from singing all night, and her lips were dry and cracked. By the side of a stream Janet bent and scooped up a handful of water. She splashed it on her dirty face and began to laugh.

She had made it through the worst part. In the forest there would be food, water, and shelter for her and the egg. She would be able to make a fire to keep them warm at night. They would be all right. Janet hugged the egg and, lying down next to the stream with her head on a pillow of grass, she slept again.

It was a long sleep, and when Janet awoke in the

afternoon she felt rested. She also felt very hungry.

"All right," she said to the egg. "We need food. Let's see what there is."

With the egg in the bag slung over her shoulder, Janet started hiking up the mountain slope, her eyes open for berries and the orange flower with the roots that tasted like sweet potatoes. Farther up the mountain her patience was rewarded. There were two large bushes of the sweet blue berries growing near a stand of flowering *Arctium longevus.*

"Ah, look," she said to the egg. "We have lunch, breakfast, and dinner all in one meal!"

Happily she gathered as many berries as her bag could hold. Then she pulled up some stems of *Arctium longevus.* "It would be nicer as tea, but I don't have my bowl anymore," she said sadly to the egg. "It's bitter raw, but it will still give me strength."

Janet talked to the egg as she continued on her way. She told it all about the heroic deeds of its mother, about her own worries, and mostly about her hopes for the egg's future.

"You will like the Hatchery. Everyone there will be so happy to see us. Maybe when you are big enough we will travel with Kranog to look for the other members of your family. Perhaps we will grow up to have a life of adventure together," she said with a laugh. "But first we will go home and sit for a long time and just watch the grass grow in the fields for a while. Oh, won't Zephyr be so pleased to see us? She'll probably scratch a few scales off her neck! And I know I'll cry."

She climbed the mountain talking away until it grew too dark to see through the trees. Weary but nourished by the *Arctium longevus* and the berries, Janet decided to camp for the night beneath the spreading branches of an old ginkgo tree. She made a small campfire and sat close to it to keep her body and the egg inside her shirt warm.

The night wind rustled through the trees, and the whole forest seemed quiet and peaceful after the rumbling earth of Kranog's village. Janet sang the list of names once more before she lay down by the fire. She would not forget, she promised the burning logs. She thought of Kranog. Zephyr would be there soon, she told herself. Soon they would all be together again. Comforted by these thoughts, Janet closed her eyes and dreamed of the long summer days and the egg hatched into the likeness of its mother, Kranog.

Gentle hands and a frantic squeaking of voices woke her. Janet opened her eyes and sat up, her arms hugging the egg to protect it. Two Ovinutrix were standing before her, speaking quickly. One's neck scales flashed red and orange with worry.

"My nursery hatchling, what are you doing here?" the red and orange Ovinutrix asked, finally speaking slowly enough so Janet could understand.

"I am an apprentice, Maestra," Janet answered, using the title of respect, "on an important journey."

"And the egg. Oh, dear," warbled the other one. She had a blue stripe on her chest that shone like silk. "So far from a nursery?"

"Aye, Maestra. The mother in the forest was wounded but had to return to her home, even though it was not safe. She laid this egg, the last of her clan, and charged me to return to my Hatchery with it."

"But you are a nursery hatchling," protested the first Ovinutrix.

"No, no, no, she said she was an apprentice," corrected the second Ovinutrix, with the blue stripe.

"But she should still give us the egg. I don't like the idea of this hatchling all by herself out here."

"I made a vow," Janet said firmly. "A vow of Gar-en-doc. I must return with this egg," she said. "I must sing the song of names for this hatchling."

Janet knew they meant well. The Ovinutrix wanted only the best for the egg and her. But she knew that it was important that she be responsible for Kranog's egg. Kranog had trusted her to bring the egg safely home. And who else but Janet could sing the song of names for the hatchling?

"Well," said the blue-striped Ovinutrix. "That certainly changes things. We cannot speak against the vow of Gar-en-doc. No, no, no. Indeed, how honored we are to meet you. I am Azure, and my companion is Orissa. Please gift us with your name, for I feel that you are special."

"I am called Janet Morgan. I come from the Romano Hatchery."

"Oh, dear, oh, dear," said Orissa. "We are journeying on our way in the other direction. Toward Canyon City. We are to assist a hatching at Highest Hatchery. Surely there is some way that we may be of help."

"Aye, Maestra," Janet said eagerly. "I had to leave behind the mother, wounded and in a place of danger. She bade me go to keep her egg safe. Is there any way to get her help, and soon?" she asked.

"I may go to her, perhaps," said Azure. "Yes. I will give her assistance, and Orissa can continue to Canyon City to tell them we have need of help."

"Yes. I will see to it that help is sent, and quickly."

"Where is she, Janet Morgan?" Azure asked.

Janet thought a moment, not certain how to tell Azure exactly where the mountain lay. But she decided to use Kranog's description. "At the back teeth of the mouth, where the gold tongue curls and the two nostrils flame into the air," she tried.

The pair stared at Janet in silence, and Janet feared that her words had made as little sense to them as they first had to her. Then suddenly the scales on Orissa's neck flamed bright red and yellow.

"Oh, dear. Oh, dear. No one lives there anymore. It has been deserted for years because of the volcanoes."

"Oh, yes," replied Azure. "How ever did you get there?"

"Then you know the place?" Janet asked, relieved.

"Know it? Certainly I know it." Azure said, and her tail thrashed excitedly. "Why, I received my training there many years ago when the Hatcheries thrived. There was a very fine school. Languages, I believe."

"Aye! That's the place. The mother is Kranog, the shining sun. She is the last of her clan to remain. She tried to leave, but when she knew she was to lay her egg, she had to return home."

"Understandable. But dangerous!" said Azure. "I must go to her at once."

"And you, Janet Morgan, who is so brave an apprentice. What help may we give the egg and you?" asked Orissa.

"Directions home would be helpful," Janet said, realizing she wasn't sure which way to go. Since the fog, Janet no longer knew in which direction home lay. And she wanted to travel in the daylight rather than wait for the guiding stars of night.

"Ah," said Azure. "Travel down this road to which we have just come. At a fork in the road you will see an old ginkgo with yellowing leaves. Take the road beneath its branches."

"Are you sure that was a ginkgo?" interrupted Orissa. "I thought it was a cedar. And I didn't see any fork. It looked more like an elbow in the road to me."

"No, I'm sure it was a yellow ginkgo and a fork. But you won't miss it, Janet Morgan. Follow it and you will reach Treetown. They will help you."

"Thank you. Thank you so much. Please find Kranog soon."

"I am going. Flying over these hills. Don't worry. I know the way well," Azure said. She trotted briskly off the path and then swerved up the mountainside.

"And I, too, am off to Canyon City. The sooner there, the sooner to get help. You're a most impressive apprentice, Janet Morgan. Who is your teacher?"

"Fatherfast," Janet said proudly.

"Ah. Very revered. Well, good journey to you, Janet Morgan." Orissa saluted her with a short bugling farewell and continued rapidly down the path. She trotted at first, and then she lengthened her neck and began to run. She blurred like a little flame in the green trees, and then she was gone.

"Well," Janet said to the egg, "that's something to hope on."

Janet cleaned up her campsite, making sure that her fire was completely out. Then she sprinkled a little more water over the egg's mossy bed to keep it moist and warm. Janet put some ginkgo nuts into her bag and added pine cones with seeds still buried between the scales. She ate a handful of berries and took a sip of water from a nearby stream. Then, squaring her shoulders for another day of travel, she started down the trail that Azure had pointed out.

CHAPTER 10

The journey began pleasantly. The day was sunny, the light a beautiful gold and green where it fell in shafts through the trees. Janet was encouraged—some help was sure to reach Kranog very soon. The egg was heavy, but Janet didn't mind the weight. She felt so happy to be able to do this act of kindness for Kranog. And it was important for herself, she realized; to prove that although she had made a mistake once, she could still be a good apprentice in the future. Kranog had trusted her, and she would not fail in that trust.

In the late afternoon Janet began to grow uneasy. She hadn't asked Azure how far down the trail the fork or the elbow branched out beneath the ginkgo tree. Janet remembered that dinosaurs measured distance differently than humans did. What was an easy jaunt for a dinosaur might be a two-day journey for her. But they had made it sound so close, Janet argued with herself. Or else she had wanted to believe it was so close. Janet studied every tree along the trail, hoping to recognize it as the right one. But they were all green, and not a yellow leaf appeared among any of them on the trail. She trudged on, her spirits beginning to grow as heavy as the egg.

The sun was low in the sky when Janet saw the patch of yellowing leaves. Three ginkgo trees leaned together, their branches intertwined. All of them had yellowy branches. Janet became excited, thinking that this was the tree that Azure had mentioned. But as she searched beneath the trees, it seemed that there was no real path. Just a thick ground covering of shrubs and little pines. A cluster of ferns gathered around one side of what looked like a thin muddy trail.

Janet stopped and stared a long time at the trees. Finally she thought she could see the faint markings of what might have been a path. She was guessing, and she knew it. It might be the right one. Or it might be the path to somewhere else. She didn't know what to do. She was tired and hungry. The thought of a village at the end of the trail was suddenly irresistible. Hoping she was making the right choice, Janet plunged down the bushy path between the yellowing ginkgo trees. She might even reach Treetown before nightfall.

A few hours later, as the sun started to sink below the trees, Janet knew she was out of luck. The trail had led down the mountain but not into Treetown. Instead of a village, Janet's trail disappeared in a thick marshy forest that got wetter with every step she took. She tried to remember her geography, tried to picture in her mind where Treetown lay, along the bottom of the spine of the Backbone Mountains. It occurred to Janet that perhaps she had left the trail too soon and was now marching down into the wet marshes of the Rainy Basin.

The land here was like a sponge. Murky pools of cold dank water lay hidden just beneath the surface of green duckweed. The few trees were tall and scraggly as they reached for the light. Small gnats hummed in the air and clung to Janet's face in a cloud of curiosity.

Her boots were covered with black mud, as was the hem of her cape. Green duckweed covered her trousers, and when she brushed the buzzing gnats out of her face she left dirty smears on her skin. Each time she put her foot down on the trail she wasn't certain whether it would stay on firm land or sink up to her ankle in a muddy mess. She almost lost one of her boots in the mud. But after much tugging it came free with a fierce sucking noise.

Janet stopped. She knew it would be even more dangerous to travel in the dark. The farther into the marsh she went, the harder it would be to see the larger pools of marsh water covered by layers of rotten leaves and duckweed. She worried that she might fall into one and get completely wet, if not actually drown in it. Since she couldn't start a fire in the dampness of the marsh, she needed to keep herself as warm and dry as possible to protect the egg.

"We're going to have to go up for the night to stay dry," Janet told the egg.

She gazed up at the trees, their limbs etched against the last fading twilight. She saw a ginkgo tree with low spreading branches. Janet crossed to the tree and looked up. Near the top of the tree there looked like a perfect place to perch for the night.

Moving the bag with the egg carefully onto her back to keep it safe, Janet began to climb the lower branches of the ginkgo tree. Her arms ached with the effort, but she kept her sights on the perch she had seen from the ground. When she got there at last she was happy to discover that it was even better than she had thought.

Two branches lay close to each other. One was wide enough for her to sit on and dangle her legs below. The second branch was a little higher but provided the perfect place to rest her arms and head. Between the two branches, she thought she might be able to safely sleep, as long as she didn't sleep too deeply, she told herself.

Sitting up in the tree, her legs and muddy boots dangling beneath her, Janet began to laugh. She felt like an odd creature indeed. But she was dry enough, and overhead the stars twinkled brightly. She glanced down at the sleeping forest, hearing the rustling of night noises and the gentle swaying of branches in the cool night breeze. It was a little bit like what she imagined Treetown to be, but a lot less comfortable. Maybe she would find the village tomorrow. She could take a bath and get out of these muddy boots. Feeling cheered, Janet decided to sing the names of Kranog's lineage. Like a strange bird, she sat perched in the night at the top of a ginkgo tree, singing the old names until at last she fell into an uneasy sleep.

Near dawn Janet woke with a jerk, her arms wrapped around the branches. Her heart was pounding, and she realized she had dreamed of falling. The sky was a pale gray, a thin line of glowing sunrise showing over the tops of the trees. Janet sighed and scratched at the bug bites on her arm. Her arms ached from holding on to the branches, and her feet felt numb where they dangled beneath her. Soon it would be light enough to see, and then she would climb down and continue. But for now she would watch the sunrise and imagine the feel of the solid ground beneath her feet again.

She stared out over the treetops and caught sight of a strange shadow gliding over the trees. She frowned and kept looking. Gradually the shadow took on a shape. It was an Archaeopteryx out flying in the early morning breezes. Janet watched its graceful movements, the long flowing tail streaming behind it in the wind. It would land on a high branch for a moment, then fling itself back into the wind to glide until it reached the next treetop. It traveled along the tops of the trees until it landed on a perch not far from Janet. The creature raised its feathery head and fanned out its wings as if to catch the first rays of sunrise.

"Good morning," Janet called.

The Archaeopteryx squawked and nearly tumbled over the branch in surprise. With some effort, the creature righted itself on the branch and looked around.

"It's me, over here," Janet called, and waved her hand. The branches of the ginkgo swayed.

"How unusual. How most unusual," the creature said. "And what are you?" it inquired.

"A human girl."

"Extraordinary," the Archaeopteryx warbled. With delicate hopping motions the creature joined Janet on her tree, resting on the perch above Janet's head. The Archaeopteryx had downy feathers on her breast and long trailing feathers on her wings. A few of the feathers ruffled up on her little head in amazement as she spoke. "What sort of human are you to be here?"

"I'm an apprentice to the Hatcheries, actually," Janet replied, glad to have someone to talk to.

"But what is that you are carrying?"

"A dinosaur egg. I'm helping a mother dinosaur that was too injured to return to the Hatchery after she had laid this egg in a very dangerous place."

"Dangerous place?" the Archaeopteryx asked. Her eyes widened, and more feathers ruffled on her head crest. "How wonderful. How poetic. How thrilling. Are you scared?"

"Not always. But sometimes. Mostly I'm hungry and a little lonely."

"The stuff of good epics," exclaimed the Archaeopteryx. "Please allow me to introduce myself. I am the poetess Anthaxan."

"I am honored," Janet replied respectfully.

"You have heard of me, then?" Anthaxan asked, her tail feathers fanned in a question.

"Oh, aye," Janet answered eagerly. "My mother has often read us your poetry."

"You're very well educated," Anthaxan cooed softly. "And what is your name, then?"

"Janet Morgan, from Romano Hatchery."

"How charming. And what an unusual place to be meeting you, Janet Morgan."

"May I ask what you're doing here?" Janet asked, suddenly curious.

"Ah, of course. Sometimes the life in Waterfall City is just too noisy. I can't hear myself think, let alone compose. Then I come here at daybreak to the Rainy Basin. I love to sit in utter peace and watch the sun come up slowly over the forest, pushing back the velvet black cloak of the night and spreading golden flames of celestial honey—" She stopped and briefly hid her face behind a fanning wing. "Forgive me. This dreary place does much to inspire my poetry. When I open my beak, I must improvise."

"Oh, please," said Janet, shifting on her branch as she tried to get more comfortable. "I love to hear poetry."

"Really?" Anthaxan asked, and Janet could tell

that the Archaeopteryx was pleased. Her wings fluttered, sending a few small, brightly colored feathers to the forest floor below.

"Aye. It's a beautiful way to greet the coming day."

"How true," said Anthaxan. "Then I will recite something for you, Janet Morgan."

Anthaxan ruffled her wings and smoothed them out beside her like the long flowing train of an evening dress. She coughed a little to clear her throat. Then she raised her head to the sky and began to warble softly. The notes of her song rose up and down as though she were exercising her throat. Then Anthaxan fell silent, and for a confusing moment Janet wondered if the vocalization had been a poem in a language she didn't understand. She was worried that Anthaxan was waiting for Janet to applaud before going on. But just when Janet freed her hands to clap, Anthaxan began to speak:

"Treed, topped to green branch
Soaring limbs above the leaves
Arms wrapped to hold this one hope.
A white moon.
Day arrives and the moon must set
Carried to the earth again.
Sun breaks open and life begins."

Anthaxan gave a little shudder as if rising from a trance. She clucked to herself and chirped softly. "Very nice, I think," she said at last to Janet.

"Oh, aye," said Janet. "It was lovely." She liked the sound of the words, but she wasn't sure what any of it meant. "And where did you get your inspiration for such a lovely poem?" she asked, hoping to learn more about what the poem meant.

Anthaxan warbled shrilly. "Oh, my humble Janet Morgan. It is a poem about you, of course. I was inspired by you, sitting here in this tree and holding an egg. From below I am sure the egg must look a great deal like the moon. But when it breaks, or hatches, then it will bring new life. Bright and gleaming like the rising sun. Now do you see?" And she tilted her head to one side to stare at Janet out of black gleaming eyes.

"Aye," Janet answered, grinning. "I do understand it now. Thank you."

"Oh, no, thank you. You have certainly inspired me. I think I shall go home to my studio and compose this morning. There will be poems of your journey and your heroic struggle all over Waterfall City by nightfall. Everyone will want to know who is this Janet Morgan! How wonderful for you to have met someone like me. I shall make you famous!" she squeaked with delight.

"I'm very grateful for your kind attention," Janet answered, smiling.

"Oh, it's no more than you deserve, out here like this, braving the wilds just to help another. But there you are, a perfect example of others first. How very brave. And what an awful place in which to be stuck. Or should I say treed? It's a pity you can't glide as I do over the treetops."

"Perhaps you could help me?" Janet asked, an idea forming in her head. "I need to know the right way to get home to the Hatcheries. I didn't mean to come into the Rainy Basin, but I got lost. I really want to get home as soon as possible."

"How dreadful for you!" clucked Anthaxan. "Yes, of course I can assist you. Why, I shall have to add a verse in my new poem about me as part of your adventure. This is wonderful!" she said happily, and the feathers of her head crest lifted with her excitement. "Here now, look where I show you the way from up here."

Anthaxan sidled over to Janet's branch until she was sitting quite close to her. "Look down there," and she gestured with her wing. A tiny finger protruding beyond the last pinion feather pointed below. "Do you see that fat twisted oak? The one without leaves?"

"And covered with a vine?" Janet added.

"Yes, that's it. First you must go by that tree. Behind it there is a path that follows a dry trail. See over there a little ways, past the hickory trees, you can just make out the curve of the trail?"

Janet peered into the trees as the sun began to brighten the forest floor. She could see where the trail curled around the dying oak tree, then threaded its way past a group of hickories, and out again past a black pool lined with white flowers. She saw the path continue, curling around ginkgoes and beyond another bog. From up here, it was easy to see the right way.

"I see it now!" she said excitedly. "And will that path take me to Treetown?"

"Oh, no. That would be entirely in the wrong direction. This path will take you to the Polongo River. From there simply follow the river until you reach Waterfall City. A few days as the human walks. And I shall fly home now and have someone meet you along the river. Will that be nice?"

"Oh, aye!" said Janet, beaming. "It would be wonderful to have company on the trail again. And I have always wanted to see Waterfall City."

"But of course you have," said Anthaxan. "It is a place of culture. Everyone wants to go there."

Janet smiled, thinking of Sada, who had left the busy city to live in the quiet of the forest. "Thank you, Maestra Anthaxan. I'm very grateful for all your help."

"Oh, you know...others first," she replied gaily. "I, too, must do my part. Besides, you have inspired me to write what I know will be my best poetry ever. Until later," she said, and began to flap her wings briskly.

Janet leaned away from the fanning of Anthaxan's wings. The branch she was sitting on bounced as the

Archaeopteryx jumped off and drifted in the air.

"Remember," Anthaxan called down to Janet, "follow the path to the river!"

"I will," Janet called back, and waved a farewell.

Alone again, Janet looked at the egg. The moss was damp, and the heat from her body was keeping the egg warm. Still, to be safe, she rotated the egg. Then she moved the string bag on her back again before she started down the tree.

"Well, my egg, here we go again," Janet told the egg. "I just hope that the trail is as easy to find on the ground as it was in the trees!"

Once on land again Janet could hardly stand up straight. The blood had drained from her feet, and now they tingled and burned as the circulation slowly returned. "Ow, ow," she cried out as she hopped around, trying to get the blood back into her limbs. She rubbed her legs and shook her feet out. When the worst of the tingling had stopped, Janet set out shakily along the trail.

In no time she reached the fat twisted tree. In her mind she could see the trail curving around behind it and going toward the black pool lined with white flowers. A moment later Janet saw the white flowers. She closed her eyes and saw the next landmark in her mind. Then she opened her eyes again and started on her way.

"I think we're really on our way home now," she said to the egg. "We'll be all right."

The sun rose over the dense green forest, and in the cool morning air Janet felt her spirits rise like the mist floating to the tops of the trees. The egg was safe and warm in her shirt. Help was on its way to Kranog, and a famous poet was about to sing songs about Janet in Waterfall City. Janet grinned as she walked confidently through the muddy green marsh. "What an adventure!"

CHAPTER 11

Janet walked along the twists and turns of the trail. Her feet stayed fairly dry as she managed to find the solid ground of the narrow trail. But the rest of her was not so fortunate. There were short sudden rain showers that fell throughout the day, wetting her hair and cheeks, soaking the shoulders of her cape. But the rains left just as quickly as they came, and the sun broke out again between fleecy white clouds. Then Janet's cape steamed as the water evaporated in the heat of the sunshine. Her hair curled into ringlets, and sweat trickled down her neck.

"At least it's hot and steamy, instead of cold and wet," Janet told the egg as she walked.

Janet stopped for a bite to eat when she found a patch of creamy white water lilies that had edible roots. She dug up some of the roots and nibbled a piece. They had a sharp peppery taste, but the skin was very tough.

"Well, I can't be fussy," Janet said to the egg. "Though what I wouldn't give for a taste of Sada's

116

sweet potatoes. Or Mammie's soup." She sighed.

Janet continued her journey until it was too dark to see the trail. That night she tried to make a campfire using her flint and tinder. But the air was so humid that the spark from the flint wouldn't catch fire in the damp tinder. Janet pocketed her flint again and, with a weary sigh, leaned against the trunk of a tamarack tree. She gathered some nearly dry leaves, wrapped herself in her cape, and tried to sleep. She whispered to the egg and, holding its rough surface to her ear, hoped to catch the sounds of piping, even though she knew it was too soon.

In the morning, Janet was very hungry. Her skin itched with the grime of her journey and insect bites on her arms and face. There was dirt under her fingernails and in the creases of her wrists and elbows. Her clothes were filthy, the hem of her cape ragged and torn. But she was determined to keep her spirits up as she made herself eat the last of the withered berries and a couple of water lily roots. She took a sip of muddy water from a pool, making a face at its taste. She checked Kranog's egg, wetting the moss and rotating the egg in the bag. Then Janet gathered her energy and began walking again.

The trail became easier to follow, and the land got firmer and drier. The soggy oaks and feathery-leafed tamaracks gave way to palm trees, huge flowering bushes, and once a magnolia tree with fat pink flowers spread over its dark green branches. As Janet walked she scratched at the bites on her arms and her cheeks. By midday, Janet felt as though she were covered with mud and bug bites. Her hair hung in thick matted curls, bits of grass and twigs sticking to the snarls. She tried to clean her face with a corner of her tunic but succeeded only in moving the dirt from one side of her face to the other.

"Ugh," Janet complained to the egg. "I'm filthy. A bath would be wonderful. My hair must look like an old bush. I wonder how far away the river is? And my feet—it would be lovely to feel cool water over my toes!"

As she hiked through the forest, Janet kept imagining the feel of cool water washing over her skin. She scratched her bites until they bled, wiped away the little flying gnats from her face, and tried not to think about how hungry she was. Soon, she promised herself. Soon I will be at the river. There will be cool water and help on the way. Just keep following the trail, she encouraged herself.

But that night, curled up in her cape, hearing the night sounds rustle in the forest around her, Janet began to cry. It was too much. Though she had searched the entire day, she had managed to find only a few more withered water lily roots and the last nuts of a fading ginkgo tree. Now as the dark closed around her, she felt lonely as well. She was too tired to go on. She hated being in the forest. She hated being hungry and dirty. She wanted her mother to come and take her away. Oh, why had she run away! Janet scolded herself. She could be home now. Happy, well fed, and clean.

Sighing miserably, Janet wrapped her arms around the egg. Then she realized as she held the precious egg that if she had not left home, no one would have been there to help Kranog. Kranog would have suffered and died all alone in the forest. And this egg would never have been laid. It was a terrible thought, and Janet quickly put it out of her mind. She wiped the dirty tears from her eyes and tried again to be brave. She had been foolish to run away, it was true. But she had found Kranog in the dinosaur's hour of need. Now this egg, the last of its clan, and a promise made to Kranog were the reasons Janet would not lose heart. She might be dirty and hungry and very tired, but tomorrow when the sun came up she would walk until she reached the river.

With this resolve, Janet wrapped her arms around the egg, covered both of them with her cape, and slept. And as if to help her through her difficulties, the night stayed dry and warm, with the breezes blowing gently through the trees, keeping the gnats away from her face.

Janet had not walked far the next morning when she could hear the distant sound of the river. At first she thought it was the wind in the treetops rustling loudly as it shook the long fronds of the palm trees. But when she looked up, puzzled, she saw that the fronds were still. She continued on the trail, and the sound grew louder. It was a steady pounding rhythm that echoed and boomed through the marshy forest. All at once a cool breeze touched Janet's hot face, and she smelled the cold, fresh water of the river. Janet let out a shout of excitement as she realized she was at last nearing the river. In spite of her sore feet and aching muscles, she began to walk faster, toward the sound of the river.

Finally, through a break in the trees, Janet saw a large spray of white water thrown up into the air. It was the river at last! She hurried to the shore and gasped at the sight of the boiling white water churning madly over the black rocks.

Janet let the cool spray gather on her face as she stood in awe at the force of the Polongo River. The noise of the rapids was deafening. Boulders and branches were lifted by hands of white water and tossed into the swift current only to crash against the rocks or get caught on the riverbank. Yet amid all this powerful motion, there was beauty. Trees on the banks bent into the river so their leaves shimmered green in the fast-flowing water. Light played across the rushing water like fireworks. And when Janet tilted her head she could see a misty rainbow in the spray.

Janet turned and began to follow the river south. Smaller streams and rivers would join the Polongo and flow into the great waterfall around Waterfall City. She traveled alongside the river, marveling at the power of the rapids. From time to time, the banks of the river were littered with fallen branches and rocks, making small, quieter pools on the edge of the turbulent river. But suddenly the narrow banks widened, and the water became very deep. The rocks disappeared and the water moved along calmly, becoming quiet and lazy as though it were finally enjoying its journey through the green forest.

Janet found it restful to walk alongside the now-peaceful river. She was also tempted to take off her shoes and wade in the water. Just enough to cool her feet, she thought. And maybe splash a little water on her face. The idea continued to pull at Janet, but she knew she had to wait. Though the river was slower-moving and not as frightening as the rapids had been, the banks remained very steep. Janet knew it would be too dangerous to go down the muddy slopes holding the egg. And then there would be the problem of how to climb up again.

Janet wandered along the riverbank until early afternoon. The river wound through the forest, sometimes stretching out wide and deep from bank to bank, and other times becoming a narrow stream of rapids. She observed that just before the river changed into a narrow stream of fast-moving water, it seemed to overflow its banks and create shallow areas. Finally, Janet decided she would try washing her face and feet in a shallow pool that had collected under tree roots on the bank of the river.

She approached a tall palm tree that was leaning way out over the river. Beneath it the water seemed still and not too deep, though farther out in the river she could see the ripples of a swift current. Her feet burned inside her boots, and the skin of her face and arms itched. She couldn't wait anymore.

Janet sat down and pulled off her boots and stiff socks with a grateful sigh. Happily, she wiggled her naked toes in the air. Then she took off her cape, pushed her sleeves up past her elbows, and rolled up her trouser legs to her knees. She checked that Sada's string bag was still firmly tied on her shoulder and that the egg was safe in its bed of damp moss. Janet wondered for a moment whether to leave it on the bank while she went into the river. But she decided against it, not liking the idea of leaving the egg alone.

Janet went to the edge of the riverbank and carefully climbed down the slope to the water, using the palm's gnarled tree roots to steady her. After so many days in her boots, Janet smiled, relishing the grass and soft earth beneath her sore feet. As the bank became steeper, she took little steps to keep from slipping down the riverbank.

Then the ground leveled beside the river, and her toes touched the cool water of the Polongo River as it lapped against the bank. Janet wrapped her arms around the egg, holding it close to her chest.

"Ah." She sighed as the cold water covered her aching feet. "How wonderful." She stood there a moment with the gentle current swirling around her tired feet. Mud from the bottom of the river squished up between her toes. Janet waded farther into the river, the water rising around her ankles and then her calves. After the sticky heat of her journey, her body felt refreshed by the cool water.

She noticed, though, that the current was stronger than it looked. On the surface the water looked quiet and slow. But standing in it, Janet could feel the insistent tug of the current underneath. It pulled at her legs as if it wanted her to join it in a game of chase.

"Careful, Janet," she warned, as she put her foot down on a stone hidden beneath the water. She slipped a little and only just managed to right herself.

Janet took one more step into the deeper water. Now the river swirled cold around her thighs. She shifted the egg onto her back and bent over the surface of the river. She cupped a handful of the swiftly flowing water and splashed it on her face, scrubbing away the mud. Then she washed her neck and behind her ears. Last she washed away the dirt on her arms up to her elbows.

Her face clean, Janet turned to make her way back to the bank. She returned the egg to a position on her side and held one arm protectively around it. She felt refreshed and eager to return to her journey to Waterfall City. Her feet had grown numb from the cold water and it was harder to feel the bottom of the river as easily. Her foot landed on a rock, which rolled away beneath her foot. Janet cried out as her ankle twisted, hitting another rock she couldn't see beneath the muddied water.

Janet fell backward into the river with a scream. She floundered in the water, trying to stand up again. One arm clutched at the egg to protect it while her free arm beat back the current that tugged at her like a branch fallen into the river. For a moment her head and shoulders rose out of the water. She stepped down again with her injured foot, desperately trying to find a piece of solid ground. But a sharp pain in her ankle made her leg buckle. Janet fell again with a heavy splash into the cold swift water. Her hand grabbed at the bottom of the river, and her knees scraped against the stones as the current dragged her under. She curled her body around the egg to shield it from the rocks, and her head went under the surface of the water. Stunned by its icy coldness, Janet was quickly swept by the current farther into the river.

Desperately, Janet kicked out her feet and reached with her free arm. Her head broke the surface of the water, and she gasped for air. Floating in the water, Janet tried again to put her feet down on the river bottom. But she was in too deep, and the ground slipped away from her feet. Then the current pulled her into a deeper channel, and her feet could no longer touch the bottom of the river.

Janet tried not to panic in the flowing water. She had learned that lesson once before, while swimming in the ocean. Then it had been a riptide that had carried her out to the reefs. Although she had been afraid, she had floated on her back, conserving her strength until her father had rescued her. But then she had been alone. Now she had to save the egg as well as herself. Janet lightly hugged the egg with one hand while the other arm reached out to frantically paddle the water. Ignoring the pain in her injured ankle, she kicked her legs strongly.

Janet's first thought was to try to swim toward the bank. But she soon realized that was impossible. No matter how hard she kicked in the direction of the shore, the current held her captive, dragging her into the middle of the river. The riverbanks rushed past her as she was carried downstream by the current. All she could hope for was to use her strength to stay afloat and hope that the current might push her into one of the quieter pools near a shallow bank farther down the river.

Janet's head bobbed like a seedpod on the surface of the river. She floated on her back as much as possible, saving her strength rather than fighting against the current. The green forest streaked past her on either side; the banks, though inviting, were too far away for her to reach. Sada's string bag held the egg close to Janet's chest and kept it from floating away by itself. Janet rounded a deep bend in the river where fallen tree branches lay half in the water. Janet looked up eagerly for signs of the river's slowing current, a safe bank to which she might be able to swim at last.

"Oh, no," Janet cried as the river narrowed. She could hear the distant pounding voice of the rapids farther down the river. They boomed like thunder, and Janet became very afraid, remembering the white churning water and the way trees and stones were slammed into the rocks by the fierce water.

As she was carried into the swift channel, Janet saw the surface of the water ripple with tiny white waves. She could feel the current begin to roll beneath her feet as it rushed over the shallower rocks. The banks narrowed, and the sound of the crashing water became louder. Janet struggled to keep her head above the surface of the water as it rose and dipped with the pattern of the rocks beneath it. She caught her breath just as the current suddenly dragged her down under the surface. She tumbled violently in the rushing current, turning somersaults as the water plunged between the narrow rocky passages of the riverbed.

Sand and grit were forced into her eyes and hair. A branch tore at her shirt. And just when Janet thought she could hold her breath no longer, the current tossed her up again to the surface. She felt the air on her face, though all around her head the water was seething white. Janet gasped another fresh mouthful of air just as she felt the current carry her under the water again.

As the current pulled Janet down between two rocks it slammed her hard into a boulder. Her shoulder collided painfully with the stones, and then just as quickly the river shoved her into another rock nearby. Pain made Janet kick her feet fiercely. She had to reach the surface again and try to get away from these dangerous and bruising rocks. Neither she nor Kranog's egg could survive this beating.

As her face broke through the white water Janet thought she heard someone shouting over the roar of the rapids. Water boiled around her, making it hard for her to see the bank. But what looked like a dark branch suddenly appeared in front of her, leaning out over a bank of approaching rocks.

With a last desperate hope, Janet lunged her body toward the branch and caught it with one hand. Her arm jerked painfully as her grip resisted the pull of the current. Her legs dangled in front of her like ribbons, but she stayed in one place. The branch held firm, and she and the egg were no longer prisoners of the rushing river.

CHAPTER 12

The current swirled wildly around Janet, trying to tear her away from the branch. But Janet refused to let go. Her hand and arm aching as she fought against the current, she pulled her body closer to the branch. She tucked the branch under her arm and managed to lie on her side over the branch, half out of the water. Then Janet heard someone shouting again and looked up. Not far from her in the river, a man seated on the back of a knobbed-tail Euoplocephalus was holding on to the other end of her branch. Two more Euoplocephalus had waded out in the teeming river and were quickly approaching her. She wanted to wave back, but she couldn't let go of the branch, and her other arm was still tightly wrapped around Kranog's egg.

Big and heavily plated, the Euoplocephalus moved through the water like small gray islands. They shouted encouragement to her and told her to hold on. When they reached her, they used their huge bodies to shield her from the fast current. In the quieter water between them, Janet was able to let go of the branch and move the egg to a resting place on her back. She pulled herself up the side of one of the dinosaurs on the rungs of a rope ladder that was draped over his huge back. Exhausted, she held on to his neck spines as he slowly moved out of the river.

"Th-th-an-k-k you," Janet said when they reached the shore.

Her teeth were chattering from the cold water, and she was too stiff and bruised to move easily. The man quickly helped her slide off the dinosaur's back and set her down on the dry riverbank. Janet sat cross-legged on the ground and took out Kranog's egg from the bag. The man waited quietly while Janet studied the egg, turning it slowly in the sunlight and checking for any signs of cracks. There were none. The egg, though a little damp and chilled for the moment, was still whole and perfect. Janet sighed with relief and replaced the egg in the bag.

"Janet Morgan, are you?" the man asked kindly as he threw two blankets over her shoulders.

"A-a-y-y-e," Janet answered, her teeth still chattering. Janet used one of the blankets to wrap around the egg to bring it more warmth.

"I am Oscar Van Meer and am happy to meet you at last. The poetess Anthaxan spread the word among the river dwellers to be on the lookout for you. We came out here this morning to try to find you. But to speak truth, I hadn't thought to look for you *in* the river."

"I didn't mean to fall in," Janet answered. "I just wanted to wash my face. And then I slipped…"

"*Jah,* the river is a bit tricky. But you're safe now. It was Bucephalus here who saw you farther up the river bouncing along like an upturned beetle," Oscar said, pointing to the large gray dinosaur who had first waded out into the river.

"I can never thank you all enough," Janet answered drowsily. She had stopped shivering as the warmth trapped by the blankets seeped into her bones. The terrible fear of the rushing water was going away, and she was becoming sleepy. Her body ached everywhere, and her ankle throbbed. "I'm so tired," she said weakly. "It's been such a long way."

"And a good job you've done of it too," Oscar answered. "Here, I have some salve for those cuts," he added, bringing out a small glass jar filled with a pungent white ointment. He smeared the cream over the cuts on Janet's legs and arms. "There, that should make the rest of the journey more comfortable," he said when he finished.

"I don't think I can walk any farther," Janet said.

"You won't have to. We're here to carry you to Waterfall City, Mistress Morgan. A good many people are waiting there to see you."

"Kranog?" Janet asked, rousing suddenly from her sleepiness.

"The mama dinosaur. Ach, not to worry. A Skybax rescue team went there yesterday morning. Now, to get you home."

"Home," Janet said. "How nice that sounds."

Oscar helped Janet climb up onto Bucephalus's wide back, and then the man climbed on behind her. He held her secure in his arms as the dinosaur walked them slowly down the riverbank. The other two dinosaurs strode beside them, humming a low song. Oscar continued to chat with her for a while, but Janet could not stay awake. Her eyes closed and she let herself doze, happy to be carried for once on her long journey.

"Look there, Janet Morgan." Oscar nudged her awake a little while later. "There it is. The edge of the earth and Waterfall City beyond."

Janet opened her eyes and heard the roar of the great waterfall. She stared in amazement at the sight of Waterfall City perched majestically on a wide plain in the middle of four converging rivers. Water flowed everywhere, in canals through the city, bursting out from wide platforms and swirling all around the base of its high walls. Huge waterfalls cascaded into deep canyons far below, throwing up rainbows and clouds of mist around the great city. To Janet's dazzled eyes it looked as if Waterfall City floated magically among the clouds.

"But how do we get there from here?" Janet breathed.

"*Ach.* This is where we leave you. A skycraft will come to fly you over the falls and into the city. It seems they have sent you an escort as well. See the Skybax and pilot."

"Oh, my," whispered Janet, excited and scared at the same time. She watched the Skybax drifting over the plunging waterfalls to the cliffs where they waited. Its brown leathery wings were spread wide to catch the currents of air rising up from the canyons below. She could just make out the small figure of someone on its back. Behind the gliding Skybax, Janet saw a wooden craft built to resemble the Skybax. Between the outstretched wings were seats for passengers, and beneath the wooden belly a man was guiding the sailing craft to the edge of the cliffs. He waved to them and shouted a greeting to Oscar. Oscar waved back. This was to be her ride over the waterfalls.

"Oh, my," Janet repeated, and held Kranog's egg closer.

"It has been my pleasure to help you," Oscar said as he gave Janet a hand in getting down from Bucephalus's back. "Don't be afraid of the skycraft. The Wing Ambassador is very skilled indeed. He will get you across safely."

"All right," Janet said in a small voice.

The Skybax had landed, and the pilot was sliding off the creature's back. The pilot stroked the cheek of the Skybax and then turned toward Janet. Janet was fascinated with the Skybax. In the air it had looked so graceful and powerful, but on the ground its long wings were awkward, brushing the ground as it walked. Small hands at the ends of the wings helped to balance it as it lumbered over the land toward Janet.

The Skybax pilot took off her helmet and waved. Janet could see that the pilot was a young woman with red curly hair billowing in the wind. She seemed familiar. Then all at once Janet recognized her, and her heart brightened at the sight of the woman's friendly smile.

"Sylvia! Sylvia!" Janet waved, calling out the woman's name.

"Janet!" the pilot called back, hurrying to meet Janet. "It *is* you! I thought it had to be you. Your name is flying all over the city. I was so surprised and wanted to come out here to see you!"

Sylvia gave Janet a quick hug and brushed the tangled hair from Janet's face. "How much you have grown since last I was at the Hatchery. You were a wee one then. And now look at you—an apprentice already. And what a journey! I always knew you were eager for knowledge!"

Janet blushed a bright red. She had always looked up to the older girl when she was a little child. Sylvia was not only beautiful, but she was smart and gifted with dinosaurs. Janet had always admired her for her skill and intelligence and had wished she could be just like her. Sylvia had helped Janet with her studies in that first year of nursery school and had teased her like an older sister. Janet had been disappointed and sad when Sylvia had decided to leave the Hatcheries and become a Skybax pilot. Janet had missed her. But then stories had come back of Sylvia's travels to Treetown, Waterfall City, and even the remote mountainous home of Tentpole in the Sky. And seeing Sylvia now, standing comfortably beside the great winged creature and at home in the sky, Janet could see that Sylvia had made the right decision to leave the Hatchery for a different life.

"May I see the egg?" Sylvia asked shyly.

Janet laughed. "Of course." She opened her bag and showed Sylvia the egg. Sylvia touched it gently and smiled a little sadly.

"Do you miss the Hatchery?" Janet asked, curious.

"When I see a perfect egg like this, aye, I do. But then I am happy knowing that there are apprentices like you who are smart and brave and love their work, just as I love mine now."

"Sylvia, I'm scared of the skycraft," Janet blurted out quickly.

"Don't worry," Sylvia answered. "Nimbus and I will fly right beside you. There is nothing to fear. Keep your eyes open. The sight is glorious!" she added with a grin. Sylvia hid her red hair inside her helmet again and climbed onto Nimbus's back. She waved and waited for Oscar to help Janet climb into a wooden seat on the skycraft.

"Hold on!" Oscar said as he scrambled down and waved good-bye to Janet.

Janet sighed and squeezed her eyes shut as the skycraft wheeled to the edge of the cliff. She clung to the railing with white knuckles as she felt the frame shudder over the edge of the cliff and suddenly glide in the open air. Sylvia called her name, and Janet, her heart beating wildly, forced herself to open her eyes again.

"Oh!" she exclaimed as she looked down and saw the foaming green and white water churning far beneath her. A rainbow sparkled in the rushing water, making a delicate bridge of colored light over the falls. High above Janet clouds gathered in the blue sky, and she could see the vague outlines of other Skybaxes enjoying an outing in the misty air. Below she saw the majestic city spread out beneath her. She stared in awe at many tall towers, houses like palaces, and bridges spanning a complicated network of rivers. Janet could just make out the brightly dressed people as they filled up the streets below. Dinosaurs, brass-tipped scales shining in the sun, sauntered down wide avenues. There were shops and fountains in the center of squares. Gardens bloomed, and huge, mysterious scientific equipment filled one square.

Sylvia called to Janet and then pointed to a tall building with a flat-roofed tower and dinosaur rainspouts grinning from the four corners. Janet looked down as the skycraft banked in the air and began a descent. It glided toward the broad flat roof of the tower. Red and green flags on the top of the towers snapped fitfully in the brisk wind. Janet saw a group of people and a dinosaur waiting on the roof for the skycraft to land.

Janet stared hard at the tiny figures and cried out in delight as she recognized the sparkle of her mother's glasses on her upturned face. Standing beside her mother was her father, pushing his dark curly hair away from his face, to better see her arrival. Beside them, her tail thrashing with impatience, was Zephyr, her bright orange and blue scales flashing with excitement in the sunlight.

"Mammie! Da! Zephyr!" Janet called out with excitement, and waved wildly. The skycraft rocked with Janet's movements.

Down below, Zephyr leaned her head back and bugled a noisy happy greeting to Janet. Her parents began calling her name and waving back. Tears filled Janet's eyes as she saw Zephyr scratch her neck gleefully and dance back and forth from one foot to another.

As soon as the skycraft landed, her parents were beside it to help Janet get down. Emer screwed up her face trying not to cry, but she gave up as soon as Janet smiled. Crying happily, Emer held Janet's face and then kissed her all over her cheeks. Then Stefano hugged Janet and tousled her hair. He coughed as though he might cry, and Janet saw his eyes redden for a moment. But then his smile returned, and he laughed with happiness to see her.

"Oh, my little girl," Emer said "My little girl come back to me." And a new batch of tears brimmed behind her glasses. She had to take them off and wipe them on her tunic. Then she looked Janet over, touching her cheek and a squeezing her hand. "Is it well you are? You're so thin. Look, you've hurt your foot. I've been so worried after you."

"Are you all right, Janet?" Stefano asked, taking his daughter by the shoulders.

"Aye, Da. I'm fine. I'm so sorry I worried all of you. I didn't mean to make you unhappy. I just thought at the time that running away was the only thing I could do. And even after I wanted to come home, we got lost, and then we found Kranog..." Janet started to cry, both excited to see them and miserable at the worry she had caused them.

"Ah, no," said Emer gently. "Hush now. No more tears. Zephyr has told us everything. All that matters is that you are found and we are together again."

"And what's more, there are poems being sung about you in Waterfall City!" exclaimed Stefano. "You worried us, Janet, it's true. But we are proud that you are our daughter. And we are proud of your courage in giving help as any good apprentice would to a dinosaur mother in need."

"I'm just so happy to see you," Janet said. "And happy that Kranog's egg is safe at last."

Zephyr came close to Janet, patting her on the shoulder, touching her on the face as soft squeaking noises bubbled up from deep in her throat.

"Oh, Janet nestfriend, sad has Zephyr been. Missing you. Searching. Happy isn't enough to say how joyous my skin shines to see you now. Safe. But very dirty, nestfriend," she added, cocking her head to better see Janet's tangled hair and grimy clothes. The little sunspot patches over Zephyr's eyes bloomed bright with emotion.

"Oh, Zephyr," Janet laughed. "I'm so glad to see you again too." Janet threw her arm around the dinosaur's neck and squeezed her hard. Then she pulled away, looking at all of them in amazement. "But how did you know I was here?" Janet asked.

"First a bath," Emer said, taking Janet by one arm.

"And then a meal," Stefano said, taking her by the other arm. "They have housed us here in the visitor rooms of the Haven of Muses. There is a bath with hot water waiting for you, Janet."

"And then much talk," Zephyr finished, her tail thrashing happily. "Oh, Janet, the singing of your journey is wondrous."

"I, too, have learned to sing a new song," Janet said. "And I can't wait to share it."

Arm in arm with her parents, and with Zephyr dancing along beside her, Janet walked toward the huge carved doors that led inside to the Haven of Muses and her waiting bath.

CHAPTER 13

Six weeks after her return from Waterfall City to the Hatchery, Janet sat on a high stool, her elbows propped on the edge of the hatching table and her chin resting on her fists. She was smiling wearily at the clutch of eggs, and one egg in particular. The long night watch was almost over, and she was sleepy. But she knew that she wouldn't fall asleep on duty. All she had to do was remember her adventure, and her mind would wake with all the bright memories.

Janet grinned at the thought of Anthaxan's poems about her that she had heard in Waterfall City. They were very grand indeed. A little *too* grand, perhaps, in a few places. Janet couldn't remember telling Anthaxan anything about leaping over rivers of lava and climbing out of quicksand pits—though it made exciting poetry.

She had been proud but scared the day Enit, the Chief Librarian of Waterfall City's great library, had invited Janet to come and record the names of Kranog's lineage. The room had been large and airy, filled with dinosaurs and people waiting to hear Janet recite the names.

Janet had stood up, nervously holding her hands in front of her. The small Ornithomimus scribe perked up his pointed head in anticipation of her first word. Janet had panicked for a moment, afraid she would forget, afraid she would fail. But then she closed her eyes and thought of those quiet nights under the stars with the low rumble of Kranog's voice in her ears. Slowly and with care, she sang the names.

At first the room had been quiet except for the soft scratching of Enit's assistant's quill and the gentle stamp of the scribe's footprints. But as Janet began to sing of the fourth- and fifth-generation mothers, several dinosaurs began to harmonize, in a long, slow hum of respect, the names of Kranog's ancestors. The sound echoed in the hollow chambers of the room, and the names were carried up to the high vaulted ceiling. Kranog's clan would not be lost, but found again and brought forward to join the present. As Janet sang the last name the dinosaurs fell quiet, only the last low notes of their song vibrating in the room. There was a moment of silence, then thunderous applause broke out.

And now Janet was happy to be home, sitting in the Incubation Room. Though she had enjoyed the liveliness of Waterfall City, Janet had realized on her journey home how much she had missed the Hatchery: the eggs, the low rumbling song of the dinosaur mothers, her friends, her family, the moist steam of the Incubation Room, and even the squeak of the old windmill.

Janet smiled to herself. Her heart was here, in the Hatchery, watching the eggs become more opaque as the tiny life inside them grew bigger.

Janet leaned down and put her ear to the shell of one egg. A tiny voice piped a little tune, a sound no bigger than an insect's chirp. Soon the egg would hatch. A few days before Grass Sweeper's egg had hatched Janet had heard its first song. How happy and relieved she had been! The small crack had survived on the shell, but the life inside had also remained. Grass Sweeper and Emer had been there to witness the tiny hatchling break through the shell for the first time. A little female, her scales a pale pink like a new rose, had piped a song to the crowd of happy onlookers. Emer had cried and then had to wipe her glasses in order to see the new hatchling. Grass Sweeper had sung deep rumbling songs of praise throughout the day, joined by the other dinosaurs sharing her joy.

Kranog had been there, too, singing with Grass Sweeper. Janet left her stool and peeked into the great resting chamber beyond the Incubation Room. She could just make out Kranog's large dark form where she rested in the chamber. Kranog had almost healed from her injury and was putting back on the weight she had lost during her perilous journey.

Janet shivered, thinking of how dangerously close to death Kranog had been. When the Skybax rescue team arrived they had found both Azure and Kranog suffering from the sulfurous smoke of the volcano. The Skybax team had brought food and water, then tried to figure out how best to bring the injured dinosaurs to safety.

Finally a rescue crew from the Hatchery arrived with wagons and ropes. Together the rescue teams lifted Kranog and Azure onto a wagon, aided by strong ceratopsians using ropes and pulleys. The wagon was then pulled to safety by a pair of Triceratops. Kranog had arrived at the Hatchery just one week after Janet and the egg.

On the first day that Kranog showed signs of returning health, Janet told her about the singing of the names in Waterfall City.

"Ah, good." Kranog sighed through her cheek pouches. "So you have remembered them all. A good student indeed."

"A good teacher," Janet had replied. "And soon to be a good mother."

"All is well with the egg?" Kranog had asked.

"Aye. It made the journey well. I've heard its first song already from within the shell. A tiny voice, but still strong."

Kranog had chuckled, a sound snorting through her cheek pouches. "I think we shall hear much singing from that one!"

After that Kranog's condition improved rapidly, as if the knowledge that her egg was safe had given her an even stronger medicine than Fatherfast's remedies. Now both she and Janet waited eagerly for the coming hatching of the egg.

Janet went back to the fire and checked to make sure there was still enough water in the cauldron. Steam puffed up into the room, and Janet rolled up her sleeves over her elbows with the heat. Then she checked the supply of wood. Satisfied that all was well, she returned to her stool beside the eggs.

She turned two eggs, carefully feeling their rounded hulls for any signs of cracking or damage. She listened to one egg, hoping to catch the sound of its voice. Mariko was worried that the egg had been very quiet lately. Fatherfast said sometimes the hatchlings were very quiet just before they hatched, to save their strength for the difficult job of hatching. Janet listened carefully. She chirped a few notes and grinned as she heard a small voice from within the egg reply.

Janet examined Kranog's egg last, carefully turning it in the light. When she held it to the light she could see the dark form within, like a curled shadow of the dinosaur. She chirped a few notes and then listened. But there was only quiet. As Janet replaced the egg on the straw she felt the weight inside the egg shift. Then the egg wobbled in the grass. Janet slowly took her hand away from the egg.

The egg wobbled again. Inside, the small hatchling was beginning to spread its limbs. Janet gasped as a tiny crack appeared at the top of the egg. Then the egg was still. But Janet knew that the egg was beginning to hatch. It would take a long time. The hatchling would push and stretch against the walls of the shell. Then, growing tired, it would rest, only to begin again.

Janet went and woke Kranog from her sleep.

"It is time!" Janet said softly.

Kranog roused herself and moved stiffly to the nest of eggs. She began to hum a low song, her voice rising and falling. The egg wobbled and then was still again. Janet moved the egg to a single nest, where its movement would not disturb the other eggs. Then she sat down beside Kranog, prepared to wait all day and well into night again for the hatchling's arrival.

During the midday meal, the Incubation Room was full of people and dinosaurs coming to wish Kranog well and to view the miracle of the hatching. Emer had insisted that Janet nap so that she would be awake and alert when the hatchling finally arrived. Though she had been reluctant to leave, the moment Janet's head touched the pillow she had fallen deeply asleep. Zephyr woke her with excited squeaking just as the first star was shimmering in the evening sky.

"Come, Janet nestfriend! The new one is hatching. Come!"

Rubbing the sleep out of her eyes, Janet quickly followed Zephyr into the Incubation Room.

Everyone was waiting with quiet excitement around the hatching nest. Stefano stood with his arm around Emer, whose glasses kept getting misty. The new apprentices clustered near Fatherfast, whose scales were blushing a bright crimson with emotion. Grass Sweeper was there, and wandering among her feet was her hatchling, Red Leaf. Other Hatchery hands and dinosaurs sat on the edges of the room, craning their heads to watch the wobbling egg. Two big cracks ran down the sides of the egg. Kranog waved Janet and Zephyr closer to the nest.

"Look, Janet. See where the hatchling comes."

Janet peered into the nest and saw where the hatchling had broken off fragments of the shell. A tiny bit of the top was gone, and Janet saw a wriggling figure inside. An eye appeared for a moment and then disappeared as the hatchling turned and twisted again in the confining shell.

"Sing with me, Janet. All the names. From the first to the last," Kranog asked. "Together we will welcome this hatchling into the world."

Kranog began to slowly sing the names of her lineage as the little hatchling inside the shell continued to work at getting out. Janet joined in with Kranog, trying hard to keep her voice calm though she was trembling with the excitement. As they were singing the fifth generation of mothers a bigger piece of the shell broke away. Now more of the hatchling's face could be seen. There was the edge of a frill and the soft sheen of blue scales.

Just as they sang Kranog's name the hatchling succeeded in breaking off a piece of the shell that was big enough to let him poke his head out for the first time. He resembled Kranog, with a bony head plate that would grow a frill of short spikes when he was older. But instead of a rust color, the hatchling's scales were blue and lavender. His small cheek pouches filled with air and he squeaked. He looked around with wide green eyes at the crowd of people and dinosaurs waiting to welcome him into the world. As Janet stood silently admiring the new hatchling, Kranog sang one more name.

"Janet Morgan," Kranog hummed, making a light chucking sound over the strange letters of a human name. The new hatchling looked at its mother and squeaked with happiness. Her voice he knew from all the others. From Kranog's throat rumbled a low chuckle of pleasure. The hatchling wobbled over to her and rubbed his face against her cheek. Around them everyone clapped.

"Kranog," Janet said in amazement. "You have added my name to the list of your clan."

As Janet spoke, the young hatchling turned to face her and continued squeaking happily. He left his mother's side and, lurching clumsily on his new legs, growled softly and clicked his teeth. He stopped before Janet and, cocking his head, stared up at her out of bright, curious eyes.

"See. He knows you, too, by your voice," Kranog said. "Those days on the journey singing and speaking to the egg. He has found in you a human mother. So it is right that your name appears alongside all the others of his lineage."

"Thank you, Kranog, the shining sun. I am honored," Janet said humbly.

The new hatchling began to wriggle, his small but strong arms thrashing against the last fragments of the shell that stuck to his scales. His legs were clean of shell fragments, but a stubborn piece of the shell clung to his tail. Janet laughed as he snorted and shook his tail, trying to get rid of it.

"Let me help you," she said, and bent over. The small hatchling purred and cooed, rubbing his face on Janet's shoulder.

"There," Janet said as she plucked the last shell fragment. The small hatchling rocked back on his tail and fell over with a shocked squeak.

"I will call you Gonmen, the swift-moving," Kranog said solemnly, giving her hatchling his name.

"A good name," said Fatherfast. "For this one has journeyed far even before his birth. And who knows where the road will lead him? And the same may be said of you, Janet," Fatherfast added.

"I am happy here," Janet said contentedly.

"But there is a group of apprentices who have learned to take their skills to where they are much needed. They travel the roads and give help wherever that road leads."

"Like Orissa and Azure?" Janet asked, remembering the two traveling Ovinutrix she had met on her journey.

"The same. Perhaps such a life will interest you in the years to come, Janet."

"Perhaps," Janet answered softly, suddenly imagining herself traveling, seeing the world of Dinotopia and bringing her skills to those who might need her. It seemed like a wonderful idea and a dream for the future.

"Janet, nestfriend. Zephyr will come too. Together we will do this one day," Zephyr told her.

"But for now," Fatherfast continued, "we will enjoy today's success. Pleased to be in the company of a mother and hatchling. And we celebrate your success, Janet, as a fine apprentice."

Janet smiled. The future seemed exciting, but it was enough right now to be standing here, among her family and friends, in the place she called home.